THE CARTOONIST

THE CARTOONIST

Richard Beard

BLOOMSBURY

Acknowledgement

The author and his family would like to thank the Royal Society of Literature for the peace and freedom of Brookleaze.

Brookleaze is a 17th century cottage in the Mendip Hills, bequeathed to the Royal Society of Literature by the Russian novelist E. M. Almedingen.

First published in Great Britain 2000
This paperback edition published 2001

Copyright © 2000 by Richard Beard

The moral right of the author has been asserted

Bloomsbury Publishing Plc, 38 Soho Square, London W1D 3HB

A CIP catalogue record for this book
is available from the British Library

10 9 8 7 6 5 4 3 2 1

ISBN 0 7475 5331 9

Typeset by Hewer Text Ltd, Edinburgh
Printed in Great Britain by Clays Ltd, St Ives plc

This is a work of fiction.
Nothing in it has happened yet.

ONE

N o make-up. No one overweight. No visible tattoos, facial hair, or over-sized earrings. No aviator-style glasses. Ideally, it's for single people in their early twenties, with regular teeth and a clearish complexion. A positive outlook under pressure is essential.

Frank Babbitt fantasised obliterating the standard application policy with an anvil. It was beneath him. He was thirty years old, an American, and a language graduate; he had the looks and the effective razor and the hand-shined shoes. He'd even mastered the smile. It therefore confounded him how anyone could ever have decided, utterly wrongheadedly, that he'd reached his natural level.

On days like this he blamed it on the duck.

Inside his head Frank had the duck, and not the mouse. They'd sensed it in there behind his eyes, spluttering and indignant, implacable, irascible, and mostly incomprehensible. It was a kind of generalised anger unable to express itself, a modern strain of madness inflamed by telephone queues, and traffic jams, and lunatic technology.

Only Frank was secretly inflamed more often than that.

He tried to keep it quiet. It was probably just a phase. He was fine, really, and if anyone thought him dissatisfied in his chosen profession they were very much mistaken. He clapped his hands to convince himself, then rubbed them together to make sure. He looked up at the fairy-tale sky-blue above the soaring domes and turrets of the castle.

Another lovely day. Then he had to leap back comically to make way for an Oklahoma coach-party, letting themselves go, light in the head after an unbelievable few days in Germany.

Frank was at the back of the castle, and needed to get round to the front. He neatly side-stepped fragments of families, some hurry-up Japs on a tour of the world, and a snigger of media students in all-purpose black. At an earlier stage in his stalled career he'd discovered a talent for picking out visitors with the duck in them, just behind the eyes, just like him. It was a sense certain people radiated of ranting and raving but buckling under, waiting not very patiently for some spectacular deliverance.

Over by the gleaming *Bluebells Ice Cream Parlour*, the duck was climbing all over the family Zamora Ascensio, from Mojácar, Andalusia, with their matching shorts and the camera lens on the Señor's belly angled at mementoes of the clouds. Their small daughter, Mary of all the Angels, was overcome with carrier-bags. Mum had bought Mary a dagger from *The Cave of Ali Baba*. Dad had bought her a flintlock pistol. And then a musket from *The Battle of Waterloo*. Mum retaliated at *The Stars Are Ours*, with a self-loading fully automatic laser stun-gun and death-ray.

Between every ride Mary of all the Angels was having to walk back along *Gran Via 2000* to store the carrier-bags in lockers, first with Mum, then with Dad, depending on who'd bought the most recent present to show how much they loved her. After one of these locker-trips Mum had taken Mary up to the desk of the central information point in the *Rathaus*, hoping to find something not on sale in the shops. Beat that. And yes, there were all sorts of extras, including small diamonds of glazed-brick she could pay to have set in the *Promenade*, just outside the park's main entrance. It was

4

forty-five British pounds for each glazed-brick diamond, engraved with *Mary of all the Angels*, and the date of the happy family visit.

Back outside *Bluebells*, Mum triumphantly produced her *Official Diamond Promenade Certificate*. Her husband, Miguel, narrowed his eyes and pulled out his own certificate, noting with a jab of his finger that he'd paid *sixty-three* pounds for a slightly bigger diamond, in slate with a white marble inlay. As well as engraving *Mary of all the Angels*, and the date, he'd paid a supplement to add *Tu Papa te quiere siempre*. Mum began to weep. Miguel said their marriage was a sham. Mary of all the Angels wanted to cry her eyes out, but not on the family's special day, not with only cartoon characters to console her.

Frank Babbitt was suffering an attack of magic fatigue. Most of the time he knew how to hide it, reminding himself that amusement parks were nothing, a bit of harmless fun. Occasionally, when it was really bad, he'd read a book and dream of leaving. But at least once a month, without fail, he liked to spend his day-off in central Paris, getting totally wasted. And, if at all possible, laid at the same time. There, that shuts up the duck.

'*Scusi.*' It was a round Italian mama, three timid children tucked in behind her, small, medium and large. She nodded her dark-haired head at the rippled moat-water fronting the castle. '*E vera acqua, questa?*'

'Sure is,' Frank said. 'That water's absolutely real.'

'*E gli operatori delle giostre, sono veri anche loro?*'

'You bet. One hundred per cent.'

'*E le rocce? Di che cosa sono fatte le rocce lungo il sentiero?*'

'Rock. The park's full of surprises.'

Frank made his excuses and escaped down *Gran Via 2000*

to the *Rathaus*, where he jumped the back stairs two at a time. At the staff-only meeting-room on the second floor, he found his colleague Herman the German already settled comfortably behind the single long table. Frank buttoned his jacket, and went round to join him, the two men making a smart uniformed pair in grey trousers and white shirts with dark ties, and the company's two-tone dogtooth jacket. They each had a radio clamped to the lapel.

Herman said: 'I've rejected two already.'

'Thanks for waiting.'

'They just didn't get it.'

'Let me guess. They interviewed like this was your standard, low-paid, unskilled job?'

'The girl was in a Union.'

'Outrageous.'

'Don't be a hole, Frank.'

Fuck you, Herman. Yes, and how about a fight while we're about it? Except Frank didn't say that because it was the duck's idea, and because he wouldn't know what he was fighting for, and because Herman the German was younger than him, and bigger. Fortunately, he was also going bald. Yuck-yuck.

They called in the next candidate.

Slim, short-haired, the polished shoes. Smart black trousers and ironed white shirt, buttoned at the cuffs . He looked very young, but then Frank felt very old. The boy had a serviceable smile, and those rose-flushed cheeks the English often had. He stepped forward hesitantly, in desperate need of some welcoming eye contact. Frank's eyes connected, then immediately slid away. The boy had a squint.

Herman jabbed his fingers together and made a study of his muscular thumbs, confident that squints were down there, although unwritten, on the corporate list with earrings and tattoos and facial hair. Frank made a second attempt to

6

reassure with eye contact, but guessed the wrong eye. By the time he changed aim, that one was wrong, too. He sighed and looked at Herman's thumbs. Someone should have had the heart to tell this person, a long time before now, that it simply wasn't going to happen. And they probably had, Frank realised, sensing Michael Miller's stubbornness, probably many times.

Herman checked his watch and stood up. 'All yours,' he said, moving out from behind the table. At the doorway, behind Michael's back, he crossed his eyes and stuck out his tongue, making himself look stupid. Frank vaulted the table spluttering and sliding, and throwing things. No, no he didn't, because the mouse wouldn't let him do that, and Frank was permanently engaged in this ongoing struggle between the duck and the mouse. Part of him believed in order, and the way things were, with the good guys in charge. Another part wanted to splutter and lisp and smash it all down.

The mouse would end up winning. Always did, and nothing ever changed, but still some of us liked to side with the duck, to fight and lose another day.

Frank waited for Herman to leave, then invited bravely smiling Michael Miller to take a seat.

The story told at interview by the majority of candidates, overheard in gap-year campsites and college bars, was work experience on the surface with underneath, barely concealed, the itch of sexual opportunism. With the right attitude there were youngsters who could tough it out for months on end, compensating long hours and low pay with the frequency of sexual opportunity: in the high season as many as 10,000 staff selected for youth and looks and confidence. Cleanliness, too. Somehow, Frank didn't think that this was the story which excited Michael, leaning eagerly forward on his plastic seat, hands between his knees.

Delaying the actual rejection, Frank explained the company's standard recruitment procedure. 'This first audition, as you probably know, is to judge your overall fitness to join the team. If you have what it takes, you could end up playing many different roles. There are, however, five main categories, all of which are equally important to the park's effective operation, bearing in mind that the show never stops. We have food and concession workers, sweepers, ride-operators, continuity staff, and of course characters.'

He drew some comfort from this introduction he knew by heart. 'Now,' he said, 'which of these challenges would you say suited you best?'

'Character,' Michael said, without hesitation. 'I want to be a character.'

Frank winced, then smiled. 'That's quite a responsibility. And it never happens overnight.'

'I want to be Cocky Chicken.'

Oh boy oh boy. There were rules, regulations. This was the celebrated *Yurayama* themed amusement-park, and all employees had to be of a certain physical standard. It stood to reason, like in the armed forces, because at the end of the day it was a question of morale.

Frank rocked back in his chair, hands behind his head. He flexed one bicep, then the other. He ought to do more exercise. He said: 'How would you deal with an accident?'

'Is this the interview now?'

'Answer the question, please.'

'I call for aid and a supervisor. Second, I'm friendly and helpful at all times. Third, I'm attentive for any statement of the guest's own carelessness.'

'Such as?'

'Anything they might say at the time, there and then.

8

Something like, "I should have seen it coming." "I wasn't watching where I was going."'

'And then what?'

'I write it down. I give it to a supervisor for use as evidence in a court of law. Should that be necessary. At a later date.'

'If you do encounter an accident,' Frank pressed on, probing for a weakness, 'what should you call it?'

'An incident.'

'What do we call queues?'

'Pre-entertainment areas.'

'Tell me,' Frank said, lowering his voice. 'What qualifies you, you in particular, to join our cast here at *Yurayama*?'

'Loyalty,' Michael said, chin lifting slightly. 'Loyalty is the truest test of an amusement-park man.'

'Quite right,' Frank said. 'So it is.' Miller was good, very good, but Frank hadn't worked here all these years for nothing. He could do these interviews upside-down, standing on his head, with his arms and legs crossed. Smiling. And humming *Only When the Sun Shines Brightly*. NEXT! Here comes the idea to bounce Michael out, rolling its over-sized sleeves up forearms meaty as ham on the bone. *Yurayama* was a fenced space with its own police force. It was a fortress, an impregnable kingdom, magic or otherwise, and more staff were always needed to search at the entrance for concealed packed lunches.

'I'm sorry,' Frank said, 'but we're actually looking specifically for security staff at the present time.'

'I have a false leg,' Michael Miller said.

He stood up and leant forward and pinched the creases of his pressed black trousers between his fingers. He hitched up both sides. Above his black shoes he was wearing purple *Jason and the Argonauts* socks, and his left leg up to the knee was beacon-yellow plastic and metal strips, like sensors. 'It's

9

the latest technology. You can hardly tell from the way I walk. Is that why you won't take me?'

Frank was amazed, the duck speechless, his soft beak yawed hopelessly open. They both stared at the leg, waiting for it to do something, other than keep Michael upright.

'I know the rules,' Michael said, letting go of his trousers. He straightened up. 'I should be made the exception. I'm a believer wishing the wish. I'm a dreamer dreaming the dream, and isn't this the place where dreams come true?'

'It is,' Frank said. 'This *is* where dreams come true.'

'Then I have nothing to hide,' Michael added, eyes crossing defiantly. He stretched both arms out in front of him, and twitched his fingers. 'I also have an artificial hand.'

B y the age of twenty-eight and not yet Daniel Travers, cartoonist, I'd slowed down convincingly enough to be living with Aunt Lillian. She gave me the spare room overlooking the street, which had a bed and an ironing-board, and against the wall a stack of soft cardboard boxes.

I threw my bag onto the bed. It was perfect. I was going to draw cartoons.

In the town-centre of Aunt Lillian's provincial town I bought red and black pencils, notepads, a set of magic markers, and a ream of cartridge paper for fine finished copies. Half-way home, I went back for a number-3 sable brush, some Pelikan inks, some Gillot nibs, and a fixative spray. I still hadn't decided on exactly what kind of cartoons, scratchy and vicious with a mapping-pen, or supple and even charming with a felt-tip, or crayon. I wasn't yet sure how I saw the world.

I arranged my equipment on the ironing-board in the window overlooking the street.

Being realistic, I then went back to the shops for running-shoes. It was for the shoebox, for keeping beside my bed for rejections, nearly misses and not quites. Shows talents, buts. I'd then have started straight away, if it wasn't for television. The set was in the kitchen, and I always had to come into the house through the kitchen at the back, because not one house in Aunt Lillian's terrace had a front door facing the road. It was their only distinctive feature.

Out back there were cracked concrete yards, and in ours a rusting tricycle which had once belonged to my cousin, Daphne. Daphne was sixteen years old and she lived at home. It shouldn't have been a problem.

Someone as slow as I'd successfully become couldn't be expected to develop meaningful personal relationships.

The bathroom was at the end of the hall, past Daphne's bedroom, and pinched into the mirror-frame over the sink was a curly picture of a baby kneeling on a sheepskin rug. Next to it, reflected in the mirror from the outside in: my jaw was too square and my brow too low and my ears too big. If I stayed absolutely still, doing none of the expressions, I was almost as stupid as I looked. But then, in their usual order, I did happy, followed by sad, and then a brief embarrassed. I did frightened, content, sneering. Confident, shy, (pause, breathe, try not to move) surprised, suspicious, furious, curious, ouch! (could do better) OUCH! Then mad, flirtatious, stunned, intent, angelic, and unhappy. Finally, eyes moist, one eyebrow raised, almost smiling: I did hopelessly in love. I could do all the expressions. I was recognisably human.

There was no specific expression for fun. At Aunt Lillian's, in the breaks from cartooning, I'd have the leisure centre, the multiplex, home video, computer games, television, shopping, and breakfast cereals. Already I'd been keeping track on the television. People having fun scrunched up their eyes and beamed their teeth. Sometimes they shrieked and whooped, a range of expressions I now began to shape in the mirror.

Aunt Lillian knocked on the door. 'Are you alright in there, Daniel?'

'Fine,' I said, shutting my mouth, lying through my teeth.

'When you're finished I'd like a word.'

12

Back in the spare room, she sat waiting at the end of the bed, wearing the crumpled beige suit which on workdays was her standard-issue armour. I went over to the window. She leant back on her hands. From the surface of the ironing-board I brushed pencil shavings and chips of rotten tooth into the empty shoebox. Aunt Lillian asked me how everything was going.

At the back of my mouth, on the bottom row at the right, I had a tooth with a hole in it as big as my tongue, where scraps of meat and onion could set up home. Also granary bread, if I gave it the chance.

'Is there anything you want to tell me?'

Aunt Lillian was a social worker and looked tired, worn-out. I offered her money for the room. She shook her head, and apologised for all the junk. 'I don't even know what most of it is,' she said, staring at the boxes. 'It's just boxes full of junk.'

'I don't mind,' I said. 'Everyone has it.'

I was eager to be making the right impression. She asked me how long I was planning to stay. I sucked on my tooth, which had trapped a supplementary plug of apple. 'Not very long. Until I've finished my best-selling cartoon series.'

Lillian nodded, taking in the ironing-board at the window, and the notebooks and pencils and pens. 'Why cartoons?'

'I like reading them.'

It turned out that Aunt Lillian had no great interest in cartooning. I blamed it on her job, and all those terrible true stories she'd sometimes tell after standing up slowly and opening a window. In the high-rises to the north of town, a thirteen-year-old boy had been found dead of a heroin overdose in one of his father's prostitute's flats. The child's body, wrapped in a sleeping bag, had been partially eaten by mice and the girl's three dogs.

Aunt Lillian shut the window. What she really wanted was to talk about Daphne. But first of all she wanted to know when I'd last seen my Mum. They didn't get on. I said: 'Not recently.'

'I should warn you, Daniel. Daphne has a bit of a fixation. On your mother. She worries me.'

'Oh,' I said. I looked for something convincingly dull to follow it up. 'What are you worried about?'

She gave me the look I was learning to recognise, as if I was an idiot. 'The usual,' she said. 'Boys, drugs, strangers. Though not really strangers because she hardly goes out. I thought maybe you could talk to her.'

This wasn't what I'd had in mind when taking aim at the quietness of Aunt Lillian's. I needed time for my drawing, and space to defend myself against a tendency to be invaded. It was a weakness I couldn't explain, not wanting to admit to weakness.

'She's planning something,' Aunt Lillian said. 'I can feel it. Take her out. Distract her. Show her some fun.'

'I'm sorry,' I said, 'but I expect to be very busy.'

'Persuade her she's not Ulrike Meinhof.'

'Who?'

My old self would have known, but being slow involved a reduced memory as well as dwindled ambitions. If I worked at it hard enough, if I pretended for long enough in the best of faith, then slow is what I'd eventually become. Slow and happy.

'Daniel, are you in trouble in some way?'

'Not especially.'

'Is there anywhere else you ought to be?'

'I don't think so.'

'Then what's up?'

'I had a nasty bang on the head.'

* * *

14

We were all going to eat together, at the table in the kitchen like a family. Aunt Lillian told me so, and then she went back to work. I wanted to refuse, but being stubborn was only one way of being stupid, and there was also the more contemporary model of making myself amenable, doing what I was told, being easily influenced. 'Fine,' I said, wanting to fit in, to be loved. 'Great. See you later on, then.'

I spent the rest of the day drawing at the ironing-board, tongue stuck out, practising hands and feet.

Cartoons were going to make me rich: they were the stories everyone wanted. The characters were everywhere, flat little superstar salesmen, and even in the old days a four-panel strip could sell, *with no further demands on the cartoonist*, in 1,205 newspapers worldwide, reaching 250 million readers. That was the truth behind our own Andy Capp, national hero with his flat cap on. The all-time champion, though, the undisputed heavyweight champion of the cartoon world, had to be Uncle Walt.

In Berlin, Mum had once invited me to a Disney double-bill of *The Little Mermaid* and *Hercules*. The mermaid married her prince, and lived happily ever after. In an older version of the same story, by Hans Christian Andersen, read aloud to me on train-journeys when I was very young, the little mermaid had her tongue ripped out. She was estranged from her family, and each of her steps was unbearable agony, all for love of her prince. At which point he marries someone else. She does eventually get to heaven, but only after suffering on earth like a mortal. For the next three hundred years.

Towards the end of *Hercules*, Mum was nearly arrested. She wanted the children sitting next to us, and also the families in front and behind of us, to know that Hercules is another European who doesn't live happily ever after. He

15

murders his wife. He kills all their children. His second wife sends him a shirt soaked in such noxious poison that he begs his best friend to burn him alive. *Poias, father of Philoctetes, light it, you useless bastard! I hurt! I hurt!*

How was I supposed to have any fun if I knew what Hercules did to his wife?

Knowledge was over-rated, but like an artist, it was best to have lived a little before expressing an opinion. Meaning you had to have failed a little, and I'd done some of that, never quite clever enough to connect causes and consequences between one episode of my life and the next. In Coventry I drew the spectators for a bootleg PlayStation *UEFA European Cup*, and some of the sky, too. In Bratislava I spent more than a year sitting in the corner of an art gallery, guarding an installation of abstract Slovak laughter-lines. In Amsterdam I typed difficult British businesses into a database for the European *Yellow Pages*, which was green.

Looking back, these episodes simplified themselves into cartoon strips, self-contained: this happened and then this happened and then this. Box after box, panel after panel, living in different places in the fragments of short-term contracts. We're mobile, we move around, and that's the way these days life organises itself. Or was being organised for us, as Mum would have it. We start and stop, ending up at Aunt Lillian's, adding up to twenty-eight.

In the space between every stop and start I was always hoping to find myself wiser and happier, but what I actually learnt, between one episode and the next, was that the white space was nothing but white. It was neutral, blank. *Me*. Open and closed adventures weren't making me any wiser, they weren't amounting to much, and somehow there was a little less me each time at the in-between. I gave up on quick and clever and special, and, lost in the middle of an excessively white space, I decided on an abrupt bang to the head. It was very sudden. And then I knew more or less nothing.

In fact it wasn't quite as simple as that, but it became simpler every time I re-told it. I'd had a nasty bang to the head. I was obliterated and remade, transformed. I was going to have fun and be happy.

Since that nasty bang, I could afford to muse as often as I liked, when not watching television or unplugging my tooth, on dogs and ducks and other comic brands. I applied myself to the basic principles of the cartoonist's trade. Every character I was about to invent, from shellfish to talking turnstiles to other human beings, should for reasons of credibility be a chip off my chippy old block. For the first time I could remember, wanting these cartoons to work, I hoped I was like everyone else.

At the very least, I'd then need two strong characters who acted the way they looked. Backgrounds should be sketched in as simply as possible, just as an indicator. Exaggerate, squash and stretch, but at all times make sure the drawing remains solid. As for the action, anything can happen. There are no constraints, not even the plausible. Relax. Have fun. It's not the Sistine Chapel. Finally, remember that influences always show through – don't panic, but do try to develop your own style.

At the ironing-board, in the weather at the window, I listened out for dogs, and children, and cars parking. It was standing up like that, between a bed and a stack of boxes, with a pencil in each hand and poised over my open note-books, that I developed the original model-sheets for Cocky Chicken and Clucky Hen. They didn't look like chickens any more than Mickey and Minnie looked like mice. They were upstanding characters, getting into shape for a likeable early career outwitting cats and rats. Cocky was cocky. Clucky was, well, clucky, but sexy too, and the chickens had their own double-act catchphrase:

'*Cluck!*'

'*I* was going to say that!'

So I had Cocky and Clucky, and also some early sketches for Stupid Cupid. Admittedly it wasn't Uncle Walt, but then Walt had the advantage of being in at the beginning, the first cartoonist on the planet to foresee the cartoon future. He'd already predicted, way back when, that cartoons would one day animate *whatever the mind of man could conceive*.

Cousin Daphne took me by surprise. She had a lovely nose. No, that wasn't it. She had big brown eyes and dark eye-lashes. Not that either. She had breasts and a belly and buttocks. That was it.

'Christ, Daniel, those shoes.'

She scraped back her restless broad-brushed hair, twisting it into a rubber-band. It was chestnut, auburn, almost reddish, like Aunt Lillian's in family photographs. In fact she had all Aunt Lillian's familiar features, though more up-to-date and hardly worn at all. 'You've changed,' I said. From both ends she pinched in at the waist. She wasn't very tall. She was the miniature of a very attractive grown-up.

'They're bright orange, and green.'

My new shoes couldn't be faulted for comfort. They were lightweight and made me feel confident of running. And anyway, hers weren't any better. She covered one of her white-soled blue trainers with the other, and from there I looked up to the thigh-side pockets of her combat trousers, her hips, her stretch-necked blue T-shirt saying *Save the*

Tiger. The white transfer was faded, committed. She crossed her arms and the soft stretched cotton fell off her shoulder, exposing a bra-strap flat across barely concealed bone.

'Tea-time,' I said. 'I was asked to tell you.'

'You've let yourself be branded.'

'Have I?'

'Those stripes. On the shoes.'

'They're functional. They're reflective.'

I shouldn't have said anything. I should have agreed with her, because wanting to please people seemed fine, depending on who you were trying to please.

She said I could see her room, but only if I took off the shoes. I didn't really want to. I wanted to tell her it was tea-time, because that's what Aunt Lillian had asked me to do.

'Mum says you're working on cartoon-strips. I've got a great idea for a cartoon. Come on in,' she said. 'You might be able to use it.'

She pulled the T-shirt back onto her shoulder, and I couldn't immediately think of anything quite so stupid as falling for my sixteen-year-old cousin. I followed her combat buttocks into the teenage bedroom, but was unfairly distracted by the protest posters on every wall (*Bad Pay is a Violent Crime*), and clip-framed covers of goggle-eyed pamphlets, most of them my mother's work from ages ago (*Free the Burgos Six! Bomb the Ipswich Courthouse! Kick it! Break it!*) On the computer at one end of her desk Daphne's screensaver said *I Fought The Law*, the words in different colours occasionally rising like bubbles.

She sat down on the floor with a pair of scissors, and took off her blue-suede trainers. She began to unpick the stitches of the stripes at the sides, while telling me her idea for a cartoon. It was a half-hour feature called *Moaning Minnie*

Moans for Head, set at a country fair where the headline attraction was a lookalike contest. Bribing her way to victory, a cute entrant from the Minnie Mouse category makes outrageous suggestions to other well-known cartoon lookalikes, who are acting as the judges. Their eyes pop out of their heads. They're funny and stupid and they can't resist.

'It starts with Minnie taking a large carrot from Bugs Bunny, right?'

Beneath the smooth cylinder of her neck a shelved collar-bone joined up her shoulders, wider than her round breasts.

'Stop,' I said. 'I don't think Disney would allow it.'

'So?'

'Tea-time,' I said. 'That's why I'm here. I came to fetch you because it's time for tea.'

Daphne didn't move. She asked me about my mother, but I didn't want to talk about that, and I didn't have to if I didn't want to. It was one of the many advantages of being slow.

'Mum said you used to be clever.'

'I had a bang on the head.'

But remembering Aunt Lillian and what she'd said in my room, I at least made an effort. I asked Daphne if at some stage she'd like to come into town. I needed to buy some pencil erasers.

'What's the point?' she said. 'It's all the same shops. Take a look at this.'

She jumped up and pressed the space-bar on her keyboard with the toe of her training-shoe, fitted on her hand, and a web page came up with dates and assembly-points for a demonstration against London's Square Mile. 'You wouldn't believe what they organise. People say they have bombs and stuff.'

'Is that right?'

'Anyone can go, but it's better if you know someone. You must have known people.'

'Only through Mum.'

She looked at me strangely, leaning her hand on the desk like a foot, her shoulder hunching up and touching her cheek. Her hip on the same side countered down, for the balance. She was working me out. Perhaps she'd already heard that for a short while, wanting to please, I'd copied my mother, living among the select few, the chosen ones not taken in. In which case she should also know that I hadn't liked it, the politics and the posturing and the grim Euro-satisfaction of knowing we could never be happy.

'How about a film?' I suggested. 'At the cinema. The new Disney.'

'Forget it, Daniel. Disney sucks out your brains.'

'Not literally, though.'

She dropped her shoe, and opened a drawer in the desk. She took out a stack of slim, palm-sized boxes, which she solemnly balanced on her mantelpiece, side-on, beneath a framed photo of my mother. In those days Mum had been younger, permanently at this same black and white demonstration, waving a placard of famine children choking on share certificates.

'Let's do something,' Daphne said. 'Let's have some fun.'

I was amazed. Each slim box Daphne balanced on the mantelpiece was a three-pack box of condoms. She said: 'Let's make our own entertainment.'

Emotion, unlike so many other things, wasn't yet disallowed. But it did turn my eyeballs clammy, like hands. For once, as she turned back to face me, I wanted to understand. I looked for some kind of explanation in her eyes, but all that came back was the glitter of fervour, in unblinking brown, and the idea that she permanently dared everything

21

she looked at. I took a step backwards. There was some sly toothpaste I'd been planning to chase from the tube, and the lazy cover of the ironing-board to set back on track. I remembered we were also late for tea, the kettle tut-tutting, the pot tapping its feet.

1. *Mum*, in a bandanna, singlet, combat shorts. She's like an older version of *Daphne*. Her placard says **Hands Off!**
In the foreground, playing with crayons, mop-haired *Daniel* as a small boy. Without looking up.
– *No, Mum, I'm not coming.*

2. Same image, except for changed placard.
Hands Together!
– *Scared?*
– *Of course not.*

3. *Mum*, leaving the panel,
– *You shouldn't be so scared of life.*
Daniel, not looking.
–*I'm not scared.*
He doesn't see *Daphne* enter from the right of the panel. She's a cute miniature version of Mum, with a miniature sign.
Hands Up!

4. *Daphne* stands behind *Daniel*.
– *Boo.*
– *Aaaaaghhh!*

Cocky Chicken stepped out onto the balcony of *The House of Frankenstein*, to survey the magic of his far-reaching kingdom. From up there, shading his eyes, Cocky could see the *Vasco da Gama Galleons*, and the ornate island rollercoaster *Rise and Fall of the Medicis*, and all of *The World of Culture* – *The Venetian Lagoon*, *The Magic Mountain*, *The Ibiza Bistro*. He put a disbelieving feathered hand to his smiling yellow beak to communicate amazement at all this that was his. In the medieval street, and on all three decks of the nearest galleon, parents knelt beside their children and pointed him out. Look, it's Cocky in his pressed green trousers and smart red waistcoat. Once they'd all seen who it was, everyone wanted to know what Cocky was doing up there. Cocky shook his outsized cockerel head, a three-fingered hand across his permanently cheeky smile, his huge egg-shaped eyes black and white and always wide-open.

Then he acknowledged his people with a wristy double-handed wave. After photographs, all his people waved it back.

It was truly, today like yesterday, a magical moment, even on this imperfectly overcast morning in early summer. An older visitor, an American on his own, joined Michael Miller the sweeping musketeer to watch Cocky clamber down from the balcony. Cocky hugged little children and looped his autograph across the square pages of their offered albums,

24

available first thing every morning from *The Casa Columbus*.

'It must get pretty hot inside that thing.'

Michael tipped the brim of his extravagant hat, and made a florid bow: 'Inside what thing, *monseigneur*?'

'Inside the suit,' the man said, glancing at Michael and away. 'Mister.'

'What suit?'

'The someone inside the Cocky Chicken suit.'

'That's Cocky,' Michael said. 'That's Cocky Chicken,' and then several paces to his right he spotted some disorderly gravel, in need of a corrective sweep. This Cocky thing made Michael nervous, and he could feel himself blushing, because in all honesty he felt like a traitor. He urgently swept away at the gravel, burning red with shame.

If it couldn't be him, then he didn't like Cocky.

It was a surprise personal failing, a flaw in his character, and the only remedy was to remind himself that up was the *Yurayama* direction. If he put in the effort he'd reap the reward, if he wasn't afraid of hard work, if he resolutely followed his dream, then eventually he'd get what he wanted. That was the way it worked.

Meanwhile, with a positive outlook, it was already his thirty-seventh day as a park employee, and therefore another best day of his life, safe at the centre of the second most incredible creation of the century. He, Michael Miller, special favourite of Frank Babbitt (supervisor), was an ingredient dissolved in the potion which made the spell, and already he'd been promoted to sweeper.

If this was a dream come true, then it was only one of his smaller ones. And he'd had to work his way up. After an orientation session at the *Yurayama Centre of Excellence*, memorising during Lunch and Learn the virtues of efficiency,

25

cleanliness and friendliness, he'd started out as a pot-washer at *The Habsburg Bite*. The restaurant was at the far end of *Carnival Street*, a gleaming strip of themed bars and restaurants just outside the park itself. The dream was in the detail, Michael had learnt. He'd taken a note that it was like the telephone, where people could sense a smile even when they couldn't see it. In his kitchen the pots could sense the smiling which went into scrubbing and rinsing. The pots then passed it on to the food, mysterious and sweet like spice.

A week later he'd been promoted to car-parking, which involved a blue and yellow quilted coat with a P and a circle of European stars on the back. Michael smiled at every car. He was often the first staff-member visitors saw when they arrived from the other world, and first impressions were a significant responsibility. A fortnight later he was again promoted, this time into the actual park, and after a few days in the background mixing linzertorte on *Gran Via 2000*, he was assigned his current role in *The World of Culture* as a sweeper. At last, a proper costume: high boots, tight trousers, jacket with frilly white cuffs and collar, and a fanciful wide-brimmed hat, made exquisite by the curving feather of a peacock. And a broom, for sweeping clean *The World of Culture* for *Yurayama*'s demanding public.

The kids loved him. He walked bow-legged to hide his limp and make them laugh, and always tipped his hat to the fluttering ladies. *Madame*. One day, Michael liked to think, everyone would live like this.

But the same women and children ignored him as soon as Cocky appeared on the balcony of *The House of Frankenstein*. That was the stronger love, and Michael was victim to an American-type weakness, in America sometimes considered a strength, of wanting always to be happier than he was. If only he could be Cocky. He had the dedication and the self-belief, and he also had faith in Frank. Frank had hired him, despite everything, and he knew what Michael wanted.

At interview Michael had told the truth, like a family value. Last time, and the two other times before that, he'd lied he wanted work experience. They'd seen right through him. They'd rejected him, but not Frank, and only yesterday Frank had stopped for a chat outside *The Magic Mountain*: 'You're really not cut out for this, Michael, are you?' No, he wasn't. He was born to be a character.

He leant on his broom, and pointed an energetic Irish family in the direction of the *Breitling Orbital Balloon Challenge*. There were four of them, flame-haired and freckled, and the younger child, a boy, had scarlet gums and not a single tooth. The whole family held hands and the children in the middle skipped instead of walking. What had happened here was that the older child, the girl, with her green eyes and fiery nature, had hit her brother repeatedly about the head and face with a frying pan, until he passed out against a garden trellis, drubbed and dazed in a personal orbit of stars, stunned teeth the last to realise, cracking like crazy paving, dropping out one by one, plink-plink-plunking like a cat across a piano. Wise Grandma O'Malley had suggested both children needed closer parental attention, and now here they were, another family transformed by one of the happier places on earth.

Michael swept and smiled. He was an optimist, with a positive outlook even under no pressure at all. Miracles happened, and behind his smile he carried on searching for the secret to making an impression on Frank, who often looked about to boil from the inside out. Careful, Michael, don't upset the supervisor. Show him how much you care. Convince him of the purity of your belief. Persevere. Michael

27

would yet make his own feet the obvious fit for Cocky's outsized shoes.

'That's the *real* Cocky,' he practised, 'That *is* the real Cocky. *I'm* the real Cocky. I *am*.'

If only the great cartoonist in the sky could see Michael now, he'd intuitively commission the storyboard to propel his humble sweeper upwards. Probably, way up high, Uncle Walt himself was already sifting and sorting, doubling back and hurrying forward, making sure that like all those other stories, this one too would turn out well.

Aunt Lillian was working late, and my miniature cousin Daphne was struggling up the narrow stairs carrying the television set. No wonder she was hot and bothered. She went back for the video, and set it up on the floor facing her bed. She closed her curtains on the dusk outside, and lit some carefully placed candles as I watched from the doorway: the flush beneath her cheekbones, the soft burgundy V-neck, the short flappy skirt, in black with button roses. Her legs were bare, and her feet and toes were naked.

Not allowed. Since the *Save the Tiger* off-the-shoulder incident, I wouldn't say I'd gone out of my way to make friends with Daphne. I just thought she might have toothpicks. Or another time, when my tooth was causing me pains down the side of my nose like a headache, I wondered if she had any aspirin. 'Or paracetamol. They're good.'

She was so young and perfectly formed I wanted to protect her, which was why I made a point of not looking. Instead, I studied her nose. It was a little narrower at the flared end than the width of one of her eyes, with a small kink half-way down where the bone stopped. It was difficult not to stare.

'I know what you're thinking.'

I'd paid a solo visit to the library. Books were undecided: cousins may or may not have been allowed. It was hard to tell because the problem seemed largely fictional, especially in the nineteenth century.

However, if I wanted to be happy I had to live within

29

certain limitations, like assuming it wasn't allowed to fall for your cousin. It was the same dull common sense as not challenging the orthodoxies of the day. Complications led to pain, as opposed to the simpler stories of acceptable pleasure, like fun, shopping, music, credits.

Instead of the sway and swell of the skirt, I therefore admired the way her top lip sometimes cast a shadow over her teeth, whereas her lower lip was thicker and also softer. Her eyelids were higher at the outside than the inside, and her dark eyelashes went progressively thicker as they worked their way out. It was the classic almond effect.

Cross-legged on the carpet she wiggled her bare toes and asked me what kind of films I liked.

'Anything really. Mainstream.'

'Desire and trouble, sex and violence, love conquers all?'

'Just so.'

'Well, that ain't what I usually got.'

The condoms were still on the mantelpiece, waiting in line in the candle-light, but this was a step too far, even for me, even for fun. With the candles flaming and the lights off and the video ready, I suddenly realised that Daphne had themed a seduction.

Her mouth dropped open. She stared at me in the doorway. She couldn't believe I'd be so stupid.

'It's not for *you*. It's for Roy.'

'Oh.' I turned on the light. 'I thought you didn't have any friends?'

'I'm about to make one.' She stood up and marched over and turned off the light. It was like switching the atmosphere off and on.

I said: 'You're going to make a pass at him, aren't you?'

'Damn, forgot the drugs.'

'Daphne, don't joke.'

'You only live once.'

'What's the video?'

She still needed to check it worked, and agreed to a sneak preview if I promised to leave immediately afterwards. Something subversive, I imagined, and subtitled, although sliding in the cassette she asked me for suggestions. For Roy. Something he might like.

A Hundred and One Best Tries. Anything with the same effect as turning on the light. *The History of Steam*.

Daphne pressed Play, and amazingly it was the opening credits of *Pretty Woman*.

'We *laugh* at it,' Daphne said, clicking it off again. 'Get lost now, matey,' she said. 'Roy'll be here any minute.'

I went back to my room and threw things about. Soft things, like individual sheets of cartridge paper. What about true love? But at Daphne's age maybe any type would do. A bout of fake love with a stranger might be her teenage idea of adult-only fun.

I realised I hardly knew her, even though by now I was well settled at Aunt Lillian's. Every morning the birds went off like alarms, and an ill-fitting drain-cover on the corner ambushed innocent wheel-rims. Der-clunk. The daytimes were all my own, but at our regular evening tea-times I'd watch Daphne sulk, her lower lip protruding. I'd ask Aunt Lillian about her day at the office, and she'd open the back door before telling us that to the west of town, out beyond the largest houses, a fifteen-year-old boy on holiday from boarding school had hanged himself in his bedroom. It was a fainting game he'd invented with some chums. It was supposed to be fun.

And I thought: if these days there's less pain, just generally, thanks to Western Europe and prescription drugs and the twenty-first century, and if we all hurt less, then pleasure is the growing problem. If the standard measure of fun stops being pleasurable, then all that's left is.

I'd never wanted to believe that the logical answer was rubber masks and tying people up. Or having sex with cousins. Or auto-asphyxiation. We all needed television and shopping to work for us, or else.

Aunt Lillian shut the door and sat down to her tea.

I didn't want to be that clever. I wanted to exist on the surface, with no great imagination or memory, and therefore appetites which were easily satisfied. I wouldn't expect to take many initiatives, nor make any great connections. I'd add fun to a limited range of expressions, be happy. It was my second attempt at childhood, with all the fun I hadn't been allowed in the first one, not while Mum knew of a single segregated bus in Cape Town, or the World Bank funding torturers in Santiago, or the oil companies raping the oceans and the womanly continent of Africa.

Stupidity surely ran in the family. Even with a placard for every occasion, and a separate wardrobe for her war bandannas, Mum had changed nothing. Except perhaps aggravating our hereditary slowness with bushels of radical marijuana.

When I was about eight or nine, before Daphne was born, I once stayed with Aunt Lillian while Mum was in prison in Belgium. We had great fun at the summer fair on the recreation ground.

'The playing fields were sold to build the mall,' Daphne said, looking up from her plate.

'I'm sure it wasn't that simple,' Lillian said.

'Simple as Simon. Every summer for sixty years the fair came to that field in this town. No more field. No more fair.'

'Never mind,' I said. 'Fancy a trip to the mall?'

Of course not. Daphne preferred to sulk and then, several

days later, the first time Aunt Lillian was out for the evening, to set up her room like a brothel. I kept my curtains open, but there was nobody lost in the street looking for a front door. I selected a fine-nibbed mapping-pen, and standing at the ironing-board I gave up on Stupid Cupid with his big fat cheeks. I worked out perspectives for Cocky and Clucky. Then, using a felt-tip, I practised the sweep of Daphne's legs.

A cartoonist's style should be like handwriting, automatic and recognisable, and it was while practising legs, in the straight position, that I discovered a chicken-leg is inaccurately called a drumstick. Chickens have legs more like the muscle of the thumb. It's the legs of women which look sometimes like the drumsticks sold with drumkits. They taper smoothly from the top to pinch in just before the ball, which is the ankle before the heel. Both can be long and slender, the colour of pale wood varnished with wax or tights.

Daphne's real legs were waiting untighted in her candle-lit room for Roy, and it hurt to believe I could hear her breathing, and the adjustment of a lightweight skirt. My tooth was worse than ever, and I couldn't get Clucky to dance with any panache. Failing, and failing again, I tidied my hands onto the bed, and sat on them. I worried.

Earlier the same day Daphne had changed her mind and come to the mall after all. She'd said there was something we had to get, and I pretended not to notice the we. 'Whenever you're ready,' she said.

We took the bus, Daphne in a baggy polo-shirt, and judo pyjamas dyed black which showed off her ankles, above the blue-suede trainers now with the stripes peeled off. She said that showing no labels was a statement in itself.

At hip-level she grasped the strap of an unmarked canvas shoulder-bag, the enclosed oval nails, the tender muscle of the thumb. If eating people wasn't wrong, the base of the thumb would be a butcher's delicacy. I wasn't thinking about her buttocks, nor the bag bashing against her hip, her flank. Instead I studied the shining skin along her delicate jaw, luminous with the growing still going on. Daphne was bursting with the life to come.

At the mall bus-stop we stepped round someone else's cousin lying drunk beside a bench. He was spat on by a football supporter in a brewery-shirt, who then jogged back to his kickabout in the carpark, over by the recycling bins. I wished Daphne would look happier. She looked so annoyed, her eyebrows curving downwards before levelling off, her mouth a thinned line.

'Look at this lot,' she said, once we were inside. There were no surprises, just piped music and air-conditioning and clothes shops and record stores, chains and franchises, all the well-known names we knew by heart, in their instantly familiar kits. 'Brands and branded. Like cows in the old Westerns. Ow.' Daphne was referring to all the shoppers in their recognisably branded tops and trousers, which I didn't always recognise. 'So deferential,' she said.

I asked her, if it was so bad, why nobody else seemed to mind.

'Because everyone else is stupid.'

Daphne looked in at the window of *Benetton*, or *The French Connection*, or *Next*. The display-window's happy ending, told mainly by photographs and dummies, was a picnic on a beach with your best friends, any one of whom was about to become your lover. Brilliant.

'And what makes you so smart?'

'I know what other people are thinking.'

'Go on then.'

' "Everyone else is stupid." '

On the posters of CD sleeves in the window of *Our Price*

the happy ending was survival and the resilient hero, after apocalypse and social collapse, making Daphne's rebellion a waste of time. They'd already bagged it and were selling it back. Buy the hat, the shades, the soundtrack. Disaffection was widely available, almost everywhere, even in *Woolworth's*.

In *The Body Shop* we could save the entire planet. It had to be worth a try, so I asked Daphne if I could buy her something, anything.

'More condoms.'

'What about a top? Or an album?'

I had some money but I wasn't a genius: it was for buying things, even if I didn't need them. If the improving story attached like a tag vanished soon after purchase, then I blamed myself. I was an offender against the faith.

'Condoms,' Daphne said again, enjoying the word. 'They're symbolic.'

'Of what?'

'The stand we're about to make for the swindled classes.'

She pushed forward her jaw, flared her small nostrils, eyebrows angling directly into the bridge of her nose. As she looked from one predictable shopfront to the next, a soft vertical crease came and went in her forehead. This felt like the event Lillian had been dreading.

I said: 'I don't think I'm allowed.'

'Sometimes, Daniel, it's hard to believe you're that dumb.'

But I was. I must have been, because I couldn't see the connection between the condoms and making a stand for the swindled classes. At *Sainsbury's*, I bought her a big box of twenty-four condoms, making sure they were the foolproof sort, spermicidally protected, electronically tested. 'No bag,' Daphne said, pushing it away, wanting everyone to see what she had. As we headed out of the shop she flashed the box at other shoppers like an identity card, a security pass, access all areas.

'That's enough condoms,' she said, stopping in the centre of the widest enclosed concourse. 'Now all I need is someone to help me use them.'

I made the straightest of connections. My tooth fizzed and my neck felt sticky, while Daphne waved the condoms in a grand arc at the expanse of domed precinct, from polished floor-tiles to whimsical clouds high-up on the sky-blue walls. She said: 'We're going to make a stand against the corporate project.'

'Are we?'

'They want to bring everything associated with human life into the market, and under control.'

'Do they? What if you're wrong?'

'Try to have some fun without buying anything.'

Even I wasn't that slow. If you don't go into the shops you come away with nothing. I went up close to all the dis-counted fun in the window of the *Virgin Megastore*, and tried to feel whatever it was that Daphne felt which made her so angry. It wasn't boredom. The town was full of stuff, fast stuff, words and pictures, names and signs. It was stuffed with recognisable proper nouns, but all of them had a © or an ® attached, and each © and each ® was like something withheld, even though this was her town-centre in her town. The signs of the times were copyright-protected, untouch-able, trademarked. They all said: none of this is yours.

I didn't like to mention it, but along the same lines, strictly speaking, I didn't think Daphne was really allowed to have cut the markings off her trainers.

It all combined to make her furious. I wasn't that angry, not anymore, but it could still make me nervous. These were the words which smothered us every day, *Tesco*, *Gap*, *Burger King*, *Orange*, *Time*, *Boots*. *Every Little Helps*, *Working Together For The Best*. *Exclusive To Everyone*. All these words and phrases were protected with those visible amulets, © and ®, and there was something forbidding about a law which could distance us from the words which surrounded us every single day. It was unclear whether they could be used like other words, those which we took for granted as unprotected and available to help us. The legal aspect introduced the question of what was and wasn't allowed, with nobody really knowing until it was too late: libel and copyright were a kind of secular blasphemy, comprising anything the dominant trade organisations personally found upsetting.

Could I use these words in my cartoons, for example? Could I use *Sainsbury's*, *The Body Shop*, *Woolworth's* as named locations? I thought I probably could, but only in approved ways, in amenable stories, and I was fairly sure that this wasn't what Daphne had in mind.

'This is bad enough,' she said, pointing out instances of the battle lost, any number of people conforming to corporate versions of who we were and what we wanted and the frankly dense, crippling idea that we could never have enough. 'And a town like ours is relatively honest. It's not London, or the countryside. We don't have enough easy ideas for them to package and sell back. As it is, they just promise us the usual beachy horizons.'

'What's wrong with that?'

'They're airbrushed onto concrete walls.'

Daphne may well have been right. In which case, Mum was also right. Both of them were equally miserable. The problem with a life stripped of illusions was that when it wasn't being painful, it could be surprisingly dull.

I went into the *Virgin Megastore*. Daphne waited outside. I bought her a pair of sunglasses advertised as an expression of rebellion, as modelled in a globally distributed Hollywood film, also used to sell a fizzy drink. Even at home Daphne called the cans in the fridge fizzy drinks, the equivalent of skinning her trainers. She unwrapped the oval sunglasses, and put them on.

'Look at me,' she said, tilting her head and looking out above the frames. 'Instantly changed for the better.'

Don't fight it, Daphne, just keep wearing the glasses. Change. Like a Tom or a Jerry, after a bang on the head, get on with the mall like a house on fire.

'Watch this,' Daphne said, glancing left and right through her brand-new sunglasses. She dropped the *Virgin* packaging, and reached into the canvas bag at her hip. 'You'll like this.'

Like a sword from a scabbard, on television, she pulled out my favourite magic marker. With the cap between her teeth, in huge arm-length letters, with majestic squeaking sweeps of her arm, on the alarmed window of the *Virgin Megastore*, she wrote *DT IS*, before someone shouted and we had to make a run for it. Daphne was laughing and I was terrified, but I'd forgotten the beauty of running-shoes. They actually did what it said on the box! They ran! I overtook Daphne, out of the mall and past the bus-stop and down into town, and I felt alive, I felt stupid, I felt out of breath, oxygenated. Was I having fun? I think so, for at least as long as I didn't think.

It wore off about half-way home, after we'd stopped running, while Daphne was still giggling and fanning herself with the bulk-buy box of condoms. I asked for my favourite magic marker back.

'Relax,' Daphne said. 'Have some fun.'

That big box of shopping-mall condoms was now on her mantelpiece in line with the others. Roy hadn't arrived, and I still didn't see how Daphne aged sixteen having casual sex with a stranger would be making a stand for the rest of us. If only I hadn't had that bang on the head.

I went along, not quietly, to the bathroom. I made a brave English face, an English brave face, and realised how afraid I was of being afraid of life. I experimented in the mirror with expressions of rebellion. Scepticism to Disillusion to Outrage to Dogged Determination. Everything was allowed, anything can happen. Daphne was a legal sixteen. I was going to use trademarks in my cartoons. I'd once made my coffee in Daphne's mug. Sometimes I even refused to clean my teeth, on principle.

I could follow my mother's example. Our sense of rebellion could be kept in the family.

I cleared my throat and knocked at Daphne's door. I went in and turned on the light. She was lying on her side on the carpet, resting her head on her hand, one hip pushed high. 'Tell me about Roy.'

'He's a big black man.'

'Oh, I get it.' I turned round and switched off the light, left again.

He blew jazz trumpet when he wasn't bowling bouncers in the local leagues. He had the cheekbones, and a dramatic hairline, and his own jumping night-spot. Judging from appearances, he operated a generous discount for schoolgirls keen to take on the world, and every year there'd always be a new one, someone who'd worked a holiday-shift at the industrial estates, making her an instant expert on social justice. What this really meant was that she hadn't liked it, and then fast-bowling trumpet-jazzing Roy could provide a subversive video, a promise of soft drugs, and the suggestion

39

that sex with a black working man uncannily like himself was in itself a significant contribution to the revolution.

Roy would be expecting nothing less than to inflict sex on Daphne, my cousin, who was only sixteen. I went back in again, turned on the light.

She rolled onto her back and mocked me, slowly closing her eyes. She laced her hands behind her head, tightening the lambswool of her V-necked sweater. She opened her eyes. 'Go on,' the challenge of those bright brown eyes was saying, 'Dare you.'

'Don't, Daphne. Don't let him do it.'

'Too late,' she said. 'You had your chance.'

'I'm your cousin. It's not allowed.'

'It could have been fun.'

She sat up, her skirt rucked high on her rounded thighs. I'd had a bang on the head. I couldn't be held responsible for my actions. 'Alright then,' I said. 'I'll do it.'

'At last,' Daphne said, straightening her dress. 'I always knew you would. But I want to do it properly. Not here. It has to be in London.'

A chicken coop – cutaway
cross-section. *Cocky
Chicken* and *Clucky Hen*
brood in a corner.
Outside at the door,
a wolf swinging
a battered trumpet, gloved
finger on door-buzzer.
Ding-Dong.

Cocky and *Clucky* look at
each other.
– *Ain't nobody here.*

Wolf shrugs and prepares
to walk away, towards
Sainsbury's and
Woolworth's and *The Body
Shop*.

– *But us chickens.*
Clucky flaps at *Cocky*.
Wolf turns back, single
eyebrow raised.

'My dream, if I'm really honest, is to work for Disney and be the Florida Mickey Mouse.'

'You have the same initials,' Frank told him, 'though without the F.'

'I know.'

'I bet when you were younger your parents used to call you Mickey, didn't they?'

'No,' Michael said. 'They didn't.'

'Go on, I bet they did.'

'No, they didn't. They never did.'

It wasn't fair of Frank to mention his parents, especially when he was just himself, or a musketeer for the day, or whoever he wanted to dream of being. It was unfair pressure when a positive outlook was essential, to convince Frank of his uncommon dedication, deserving of rapid promotion.

'I'm sorry,' Frank said, 'I didn't mean to upset you.'

'They used to call me Mouse, actually.'

Frank contemplated hitting him over the head with a huge wooden mallet, to knock some sense into him. He'd offer him a dynamite sandwich and steal away, smirking, but then the duck's remedies were never very helpful.

Inviting Michael Miller into Paris was an impulse Frank Babbitt was regretting at leisure. They were stuck near the end of a mid-afternoon queue for the Louvre, stretching back into the courtyard with the famous glass pyramid. The weather was an early-summer selection: sunshine, high scudding clouds, occasional flurries of wind, and Michael wasn't impressed. Paris was also woefully short on pedestrian walkways, snackfood outlets, and rubberised children's play areas. It had exposed power lines and lethal speeding traffic. The queues for its main attractions moved unforgivably slowly, and offered no information about how long you'd have to wait.

'Yes,' Frank said, 'point taken. But in Paris I can get completely wasted, and sleep with strangers.'

'But apart from that?'

'I'm allowed to be sad for as long as I like.'

'I'm never sad.'

Frank didn't believe that Michael Miller's weird eyes made him a weird person. Straight eyes, the type most people had, were a brilliant free gift. They meant nothing more than great legs, or elegant fingers, except that eyes were thought to be more important than that. Frank didn't buy it. However, Michael's deep and probably insane conviction that all his dreams could come true, now that was convincingly weird.

'We don't necessarily have to queue,' Michael said. He stood on tiptoe and strained his neck to look over the heads of the people in front. He saw many more heads.

'I think we do,' Frank said. 'If we want to get in. If you live near Paris you have to visit the Louvre. Those are the rules.'

'I'm just saying we don't have to wait if we don't want to. We could magic our way in.' He crossed his good arm over the other, and Frank still couldn't predict which of Michael's eyes was most likely to be looking back at him. Embarrassed when he was wrong, he glanced at Michael's hand. It looked unbelievably real, apart from something odd in its reflection of light. The fingernails were too uniform, perhaps, and

43

didn't separate at the ends from the skin, or the plastic or whatever. As for his false leg, he maybe had a slight limp, but nothing Frank would normally have remembered.

It was something else, far more important, that Frank had recognised about Michael. He was definitely a mouse man. He had that kind of certainty about him, knowing exactly where he was going even if it was difficult to get there, expecting inanimate objects and all God's creatures to bend and sing to help him on his way. This was Michael's particular type of innocence, and Frank found he liked him for it, especially as these days mice men weren't as widespread as they used to be. Ducks were much more common.

'You don't believe in magic, do you, Frank?'

'Sanity is precious, Michael.'

'If you don't believe in it, it can't happen. *Those* are the rules.'

Inviting Michael into Paris to re-acquaint him with reality seemed like an essentially humane service, though Frank couldn't say exactly why. It felt worthwhile for its own sake, just like his initial decision to actually employ him. Ah, the look on Herman's face! Frank had felt virtuous, decisive, reinforcing the human at the centre of his wavering being. By hiring Michael he'd personally made something unlikely but wished-for come true, almost like magic, and for Frank it had been a rare opportunity to try out the magician's hat. He didn't like to imagine how unmagical a world Michael must have come from, to lose a hand and a leg, to think that dressing up as a cartoon favourite would somehow make everything better again.

Michael refused to talk about the past. He said that inside their amusement-park it was irrelevant, as if he'd been born fully-formed on the moat-bridge of the *Yuraya-*

44

ma castle. He glanced across at Frank, expecting him to be impressed.

The queue moved. It stopped again. Michael compared it unfavourably with queues at home. *Home*, and Frank was reminded why Michael needed pastis, for his own good, and an introduction to the curved light under Parisian bridges, and the enchantments of the mustard-grey Seine. He needed beguiling with all the rival images on offer at the Louvre, of other lives, elsewhere and at other times, because Frank's newest noble ambition was to save Michael from himself.

Michael was wearing a glitter and scarlet *Clucky Anniversary* sweatshirt, and new blue jeans from *Yurayamode Accessories*. As the queue shuffled forward, stopped, shuffled, Frank tried again for Michael's life before the park. 'Tell me about your parents.'

He'd been born in a forest, with only his mother to care for him. As a child, he'd gone to stay with his father in a tiny Italian village, where they'd lived above the workshop. Michael was almost breathless with good intention.

'You come from Oldham in England. It was on your application form.'

Michael's only true home was an abandoned mansion with no friends but the crockery. To tell the truth, he said, he loved all the animals, walking and talking. He started to hum show-tunes, from *Lucky Clucky Comes Home*.

Frank suggested, as patiently as he could, that it wasn't unusual to have an unamusing-type past before the amusement-park. In fact he had one himself. At school he'd read too many novels, and fantasised dark rain and meaningful overcoats. He'd dreamt of being cold and unreliable on the continent of Europe, as proof that he had a soul.

Michael listened closely. He already knew the story ended

happily, with Frank as a supervisor in the *Yurayama* theme-park.

'Just my luck,' Frank said. 'Born in California.'

He learnt to surf. He read self-help books. After graduating from college he drove a pick-up to Los Angeles to look for work as an actor. He found out after many auditions that he was usually good enough to nearly miss, a doomed level of talent, and a truth he was accepting badly at a time when the trade press first publicised auditions for the newly opened *Eurodisney* near Paris. They were recruiting in America because by the summer of 1993, only sixteen months after opening, the park had lost half its original 12,000 workers. This was the fault of highly complex global economic factors. Meaning it was all the fault of Europeans. Where were they? What did they do for fun? They weren't the same over there, and threatened to ruin everything.

For some time Frank continued to nearly miss and not quite and show talent but, all while slowly falling for the dream of Frank Babbitt playing the real-life role of a melancholy American near Paris. By that time, *Eurodisney* had become *Disneyland Paris*. Drinking and smoking were now allowed, and no new staff were needed. Fortunately, in a triumphant performance in an office near Santa Barbara, he breezed the audition for one of Disney's competitors, the recently completed *Yurayama*. He came over and he stayed, and then he stayed some more. He didn't tell Michael how at his age, still to be stuck as a supervisor, in uniform, was like being poisoned and paralysed in a web, acting compliantly when he felt like acting up. Nor did he mention the duck.

'You're so lucky,' Michael said. 'I wish I could be you.'

'I also have parents,' Frank said, relentlessly. He wanted Michael to admit to another world as well as this one, in

46

which we all have a past, and where people live differently. 'Tell me about your family back in England.'

'Shall we go to the front now?'

Michael rolled the leg of his jeans above the knee. He leant his weight against Frank and unclipped his lower leg, its yellow plastic and metal sensors plunged inside a powder-blue *Flying Dr Faustus* sock, itself disappearing inside a round-toed, soft-soled shoe. He handed the combination foot and leg to Frank.

'Magic,' he said, hopping sideways, his empty trouser-leg falling and flapping. 'Now let's skip the queue.' He steadied himself against Frank's shoulder, then hopped the length of the line to the front. There was a special entrance marked disabled, and they went straight through. Michael took back his leg.

'All you have to do is believe,' he said, looking up as he clipped it back on. His eyes were wayward in a cross-fire of certainty.

Frank was furious with him for not having done it sooner. Determined not to waste any more time, he grabbed Michael's arm and walked him straight to the main event, not expecting everyone else to have had much the same idea. Inside the gallery a second queue had formed, this time for the *Mona Lisa*. Frank's duck threw down his hat.

Thankfully, this queue moved more quickly, because the people at the front were often disappointed. The attraction was too small. It didn't move. What did it actually do?

'Look at the background,' Frank whispered, when they'd made it up close. 'See everything that's happening behind her back.'

'I'm looking,' Michael said, leaning his head one way, then the other. He held the restraining hip-height rope in both hands.

47

'Which is better,' Frank asked him, 'this, or an original drawing of Mickey Mouse? Take your time. It's not for a magazine.'

'How much is this one worth?'

'Not important.'

'People say a thousand words,' Michael said, peering more closely.

'What?'

'They say a picture's worth a thousand words. Cartoon animators fit sixteen pictures into every foot of film.'

'Not now, Michael.'

'The film runs at ninety feet a minute, so in a feature one hundred minutes long we have 144,000 separate pictures. In *Pinocchio* there are half a million. At a value of a thousand words a picture that single film is therefore worth 500 million words. Try reading *that*.'

'It's not a competition. The *Mona Lisa*, Michael. Tell me about this picture.'

'It's only one picture. What can I say?'

He turned and pushed an exit through the people bunched in behind him. Frank followed, strangely jealous of Michael's sense of certainty. Strong drink ought to fix him. Strong drink and women caused reliable damage. Frank therefore agreed that Michael was right, and the Louvre was nothing but still lives, dead painters. Fortunately, he knew a bar.

'I'd like to see Notre-Dame.'

'It's a great bar,' Frank said, bustling and cajoling, guiding Michael skilfully through stalled traffic and along the peopled pavements. 'Very French. Very Parisian. Everything you'd imagine it to be.' It was dark wood and a scratched zinc counter, with beer pumps and Calvados bottles fronting a mirror-backed muddle of white-bloused waitresses. The

48

customers were full-colour life-models, artists, anarchists. Occasionally they were single women.

While he gabbled on, Frank noticed that even in Paris he'd lost none of his talent for identifying the duck. It took them some time to work their way round a queue for the lift to the highest platform of the Eiffel Tower.

'That would make a half-decent ride,' Michael said, looking up, shading his eyes.

Frank, however, was more interested in a standard mother-and-child combination close to the front of the queue. Northern Europe, most likely, the mother something in Social Research, say near The Hague, and look at her – she was fuming! Her six-year-old daughter Mieke was wearing beribboned Minnie ears and listening on her walkman to *Bibbidi Bobbidi Bach*, while Mum was thinking Jesus, I tried to keep it out, so how did the mouse get into the house?

She blamed, in no particular order, the kids at school swapping merchandised lunch-box items, a Minnie Mouse cycle helmet from an ignorant uncle as a sixth-birthday present, the posters on the Arnhem to Zwolle highway – *Hoe u hier komt – de magie Mickey is dichterbij dan u denkt!* – the unavoidable clips on television, breakfast cereals, yoghurts, bathmats, toothbrushes. Realistically, the mouse couldn't be kept out. Wherever you are, it's already in.

A girl from the year above had swapped little Mieke one pair of second-hand Minnie ears for one pair of brand-new snow goggles, but Mum was unmoved. Their week in Paris, organised a long time in advance and at no little expense, was intended to broaden their cultural horizons. It was most certainly not a trip to *Disneyland Paris*, even though Mieke swore she'd spend Christmas with Daddy if they left without meeting Minnie.

'We're not meeting Minnie.'

'Or *Yurayama*. We could go there instead. I could meet Clucky.'

'I said no.'

'But I *love* her!', and Mum was already hating herself for wondering how much a day of *Yurayama* would cost, maximum.

Michael Miller saw the same girl in her Minnie Mouse ears, and he pointed her out. She'd be having much more fun at one of the theme-parks, and so would her fretful mother, far from the passing disaster of emergency sirens, and wild teenagers on skates, and unpredictable North Africans pushing beaded bracelets and amphetamines and woven leather belts.

Frank's bar was some distance further on, and when they finally arrived he settled Michael into the quietest corner, and asked him what he'd have.

'I don't drink.'

The raging duck spun his fists, then leapt up and down on his hat. Frank elbowed him aside, and stoically explained that drinking pastis in Paris was an attraction as well known and highly regarded as any rollercoaster the world over. Everyone should try it at least once.

He caught the attention of a waitress, and while she fetched the drinks Frank was tempted, not for the first time, to drift between tables asking other customers if he didn't recognise them from somewhere. There was a definitive Jack Kerouac writing by the window, and Josephine Baker at the bar with some students of '68. There was a pale exposure of New Wave starlets, and all the usual Hemingways.

Michael sipped at his first-ever pastis, and made a face. Frank added the water, and before long was buying him his second. Michael bought the third with his own money. 'Now

50

that's what *I* call magic,' Frank said, cheering up. 'How would you like to make some new friends?'

As afternoons became evenings in bars like this one, Frank always remembered how much respect he had for women. Summer was coming and skin was the in-thing, disguised and disclosed. He ought to talk to them more. This thought invariably encouraged him to get drunk enough to try it, and continuing Michael's education, Frank informed him that the secret with women was in the theming. Out of habit, and a sense of expatriate tradition, Frank usually introduced himself as an American in Paris, yes actually, working on an autobiographical novel.

'No you're not.'

'Yes I am, Michael.'

'You said you were really an actor.'

'It's a theme. I'm only saying I'm a writer to make an impression on people.'

'What people?'

'Women people.'

As a writer Frank was brilliant but tortured, creative but unproductive, ripe for the sexual saving. He wore all-over corduroy. 'It's just a question of stringing together a few recognisable messages, as a kind of personality shortcut. Think of it as a way of speeding things up.'

Michael, clearly a little drunk, wondered how this connected with moonlight, and romance. What about the duets, and the dancing, and the wry approval of the wise old owl in the harmonising trees? 'Couldn't you just talk to them normally? Why not impress them with good sense and generous fellow-feeling?'

'You live in a dream world, Michael. Watch and learn.'

Up at the bar Frank soon had a tawny Swedish twin sympathising with his selfless struggle against the ruthless

Manhattan publishing mafia. He was also having thematically accurate trouble with movie agents, the dogs.

Behind him, Michael was making an acceptable start with the sister, confiding that he'd run away from the circus after they'd locked his mother in a truck. It was her punishment for attacking the other elephants. His Swede had a good laugh at that.

Frank moved over to a girl with gorgeous bronzed skin, who was about his height and really very lovely. She was French, and her name was Jeanne, and she was one of the world's few expert dress-wearers, and if Frank didn't sleep with her he'd surely die. She didn't like books. Frank was a resting conceptual installation artist. He was wearing a silver suit and several layers of button-down shirts.

A scuffle broke out behind them. 'Nej, nej, nej!', a woman's voice, and then, in accented English: 'Don't be *bananas*!' Frank turned in time to see the girl's drink dripping from Michael's face, and several Hemingways at the bar perking up at the possible theme of a punchy grace-under-pressure rescue of a distressed Swedish damsel. Frank told dark-haired, golden-skinned Jeanne the dress-wearing woman of his dreams that she was not to leave under any circumstances. He wouldn't be gone long.

'I only asked her if she wanted to dance,' Michael complained, brushing beer off the front of his branded sweatshirt. Frank ushered him back to their original corner.

'You're drunk.'

'A waltz. It works first time in the films.'

'They're cartoons, Michael.'

'I know,' he said. 'I'm sorry. I ought to have known that.'

Still blinking, he said several times how sorry he was. It must have been the drink. 'Frank, you're my only friend. I didn't mean any harm by it.'

'Michael, you're an idiot.'

'I said I was sorry.'

He stretched out his hand, and as Michael Miller's saviour, Frank wondered if it was possible that Michael was already saved. He was wanting Frank to shake hands, as a sign of friendship, and apology, and as a small gesture acknowledging that Frank was invariably right. From now on Michael would be making an effort to appreciate the *Mona Lisa*, and the unpredictable Africans, and these lightning weekend raids on the wine-and-women realities of Paris. He'd agree to forget all theme-parks, at least for the rest of the evening, so proving yet again that after enough pastis almost everything was possible.

Frank was therefore proud to take Michael Miller's hand, as a binding agreement on all-round sanity from now on in. They shook, Michael squeezed, and then Frank couldn't move his fingers. They were stuck together in Michael's rigid artificial grip.

'Stop it, Michael.' Frank focused on the eye on the right, which was suddenly still, staring. It was glassy, brittle but hard.

'I've had too much drink to drink.'

'It's early yet. Let's have another.'

'Much too much. There was something I wanted to say.'

'Michael, my hand, you're crushing it.'

'I want to be a character.'

'I gave you a job, Michael, didn't I give you a job in *Yurayama*?'

'As a sweeper.'

'I invited you into Paris. I'm your friend. Be realistic.'

'I have squinty eyes. I'm a peg-leg. If I was a super-hero they'd call me The Plastic Hand. I know all that. I'm not a big fan of the real world.'

'Michael, you're hurting me. Ow.'

Frank thought he felt a bone crack, but it was probably just shifting into a better position to crack in a minute. With his free hand he tried to prise away Michael's cold fleshlook fingers, but he couldn't shift them. He looked over his shoulder, but nobody was planning his rescue. 'You know it won't make any difference?'

'What won't?'

'Dressing up in a chicken suit.'

'I'll believe whatever I want,' Michael said. 'Nobody can stop me.'

'Right,' Frank said. 'Sure. I just thought you'd like to see something different. Michael, let go. Please. We'll have another drink. We'll go to a club.'

'I want to be Cocky Chicken.'

'It doesn't work like that. Michael, you're breaking my hand. It hurts. Michael, please.'

Frank had started to sweat, his forehead, his armpit, but still Michael held on. 'I *badly* want to be Cocky Chicken,' and Frank remembered being bullied like this at school. He wasn't a child. In Paris of all places he wouldn't be treated like a child.

'You can be Cocky Chicken.'

Michael didn't let go.

'I said you can be the Chicken, Michael. You can be Cocky.'

'Promise?'

'I said so, didn't I?' He'd dress Michael up in the chicken suit and life would stay the same and then he'd be sorry.

Michael let go. Frank shook his hand about and blew on the knuckles, looked for bruising, stuck his fingers under his arm. He also looked round to check on Jeanne, who waved and winked at him. He managed a smile as she rippled in the expert dress.

'Time to leave,' Frank said, rubbing the blood back through his fingers.

'Where are we going?'

'I'm not going anywhere.'

The duck was stepping forward, hands on hips, webbed foot toe-tapping, taking responsibility. Move along, buschter, lightsch out. 'You were just about to leave, Michael. On your own.'

'Was I?'

'You were.' And good riddansch.

Frank shadowed him towards the door, staying safely on the side of the real and weaker hand. He was ably backed up by the beetled brow and protruding elbows of the indignant duck.

'What about getting home?'

'You'll be fine.' He could squeeze himself out of trouble with his bionic fingers.

'I don't know the way.'

'Ask someone.'

At the door, which Frank held open, Michael said: 'Frank? Don't forget you promised.'

Frank pushed him outside, and in the duckish version of life without limits he blew a sustained raspberry and slammed the door on a job well done. In fact Michael lingered, and Frank had to shoo him away, for his own safety (all those itchy Hemingways). He closed the door gently, so as not to cause offence.

Back at the bar he puffed out his matelot chest and clapped together his antic, three-fingered hands. Now, where was I?

Jeanne was laughing with a young Chinese, who'd been dealing out flyers for a late-night cabaret so hilarious they had to employ a doctor. There was also a rumour that the club's owner was a veteran of the Vietnam war, the next best thing to Hemingway himself.

Jeanne said: 'How about it?'

Paris could be so uniquely wonderful.

Frank left the bar with Jeanne. No sign of Michael. They followed the bare legs and backs of the Swedish twins, and just for a moment Frank walked the way the girls walked. He cleared his throat, and once more he was an American in Paris, working on a novel. And this time he really believed it. He felt special, and made a point of telling Jeanne she was also special. We are *all* special, he said. Then he asked Jeanne if she didn't just love this town.

'Actually,' she said, 'I often dream of being elsewhere.'

Frank told her he was always elsewhere, and similar easy touches, and in the next panel they arrived at the club.

It was downstairs from a narrow street-level bar, a long underground cellar packed with tables, people sitting and standing, many of them Chinese. There was a stage at the far end, with footlights picking out angles in descendant layers of smoke. Helium balloons bumped amiably along the arched cellar-ceiling, and stamped on each of their tight reflective skins was a pair of amazed oval eyes, the unavoidable beaky grin.

Frank groaned, but at least he had Jeanne, her shoulder naked against his shoulder. They lined up with their backs along the bar, the last to arrive before the show. The lights dimmed. The PA played an instrumental *These Fowlish Things*, calming down the house. All quiet now. Then the blash of the French cancan and spotlights and here we go, a counterfeit Cocky bounding across the stage, elbows high, mad world-wide smile, milking the spontaneous applause. And kick! Welcome to plump Cocky Chicken's big night out.

Frank took a professional interest. None of this was licensed. He assumed it was satirical. It was definitely underground, and disallowed by law. He found fault in the crucial department of the beak. This was Cocky's defining characteristic, immediately recognisable even in silhouette, on the side of the smallest packet. This counterfeit Cocky had a beak slightly out of shape, from too much late-night roistering. There was also a visible breathing hole at the back of the open red mouth, but when the cancan came to an end Frank clapped like everyone else, Jeanne as gleefully as anyone.

A Chinese waitress dressed as a French maid started collecting the helium balloons, and when Frank's elbow fell off the bar Cocky covered his mouth and shook his head. Fuck off, Cocky. Frank ordered another drink.

The waitress floated the balloons she'd collected to the ceiling at the front of the smoky stage, their foil strings hanging down like a flimsy glittering curtain. Another blash of cancan, and two Cluckys in short-skirted blue and yellow polka-dot dresses and heeled yellow shoes bounded out across the stage, arm in arm and high-kicking to the frantic music. Then two more fresh Cockys, to loud applause. They were everywhere. The first Cocky made a big performance of hushing the four new arrivals, until eventually they all stood quietly, legs crossed, feathered gloves up coyly, waiting. The leader then selected four balloons, and handed out one each to the two identical pairs of Cocky and Clucky behind him. Turning again to face the audience, reaching inside the pocket of his waistcoat, he then showily produced an over-sized pin. He plucked down a balloon from the ceiling, and pulled up a microphone from the waitress. He popped his own balloon, and sucked in the helium.

'POWWWWW!' His high-piped voice took a dying fall. He inhaled more gas, and his mouse-child voice leapt straight back up there. 'Right Between the Whiskers!'

The sugar rush of an accelerated showtime medley, and the chickens energised for some formation in and outs. They

57

all popped their balloons and breathed in, and helium-voiced they sang a re-worded adult arrangement of *Cockle-doodle-don't-my-baby*. Whenever one of their voices began to crack, to the greater hilarity of the pointing, laughing, Gauloises-smoking Chinese, the chicken in question would make a hammed-up grab for a new balloon. Pop and inhale. *Powwwww! Right Between the Whiskers!*

The show reminded Frank of work, and made him miserable. Jeanne was loving it, clapping along to the songs, swaying against him, not realising that all Frank wanted was some good clean fun, like instant sex beneath her accessible dress. He wondered what Michael would have made of it. He'd have called the police. He'd have strangled the cast and most of the audience with his animatronic robohand.

Frank turned to the bar, but instead of ordering another drink it occurred to him, suddenly, surprisingly, beyond the fluster of the duck, that what he wanted was something to take seriously. He lived surrounded by fun. And when it wasn't fun it was irony or indifference, or the hilarious farce of casual sex. It seemed there was nothing that couldn't be laughed at, and they wanted him to laugh at everything.

Like a spell broken, he stopped believing he was surrounded by happening actors and hotshot models, and glamour-survivors from vicious Asian wars. Not everybody needed to escape themselves with the simplest versions of their favourite stories. However great the pressure, he didn't have to live like a cartoon. He even began to doubt that he'd be spending the rest of his life with Jeanne, and her closet of impeccable dresses. It seemed easier to leave.

He didn't say goodbye, not to Jeanne, nor to any of the others he'd earlier imagined sleeping with. Instead, he used his hands to lie some internationally recognised sign-language, meaning back soon, as soon as possible, and slipped upstairs just as the Cockys and Cluckys stamped into a sword-dance on the American flag, scuffed on the wooden stage beneath those furious synthetic shoes.

S ix a.m. at the central bus station, watching Daphne walk. She laughed out loud, her breath escaping silver across the numbered coach-bays, up through the chill night sky. She threw back her head, auburn hair jostling her shoulders, cheeks raised high and eyes creased closed. I took a fully automatic photograph, of her throat.

'You', she said, and the almond brightness of her daring brown eyes made her look southern, Spanish, 'are wearing the most ridiculous pair of trousers I've ever seen.'

She smiled and licked her teeth. Then she came over and kissed my cheek, and my body raced ahead of itself, sending back improbable messages to the brain. By the time my brain caught up the body was already out there, walking on thin air, glorious and buoyant and about to look down.

I yanked myself back to solid ground, at the edge of the cliff. I wasn't going to make the same mistake twice. According to Daphne I'd agreed to make a stand against the corporate project, and only a total idiot would ever have thought she'd meant anything else.

'And you,' I said. 'And you too.'

Her trousers weren't half as ridiculous as mine. This was her big plan and she'd worked it all out, and it had nothing to do with sex. So she said. Instead, she'd insisted that for both of us it had to be wide-legged trousers which crumpled over the shoes, without yet explaining why. For herself she'd found some loose-fitting denim dungarees, almost fashionable, with the faded bib and shoulder-straps straight-lining her ribbed black polo-neck. As instructed, I'd bought a foolproof automatic camera at the same time as these apparently ridiculous Samaritans slacks, in beige. I'd later unstitched the inside-linings of the pockets, before fixing them together again with safety-pins.

She'd promised it was going to be fun. Aunt Lillian was happy because Daphne was getting out more. Naturally I took the credit, measurable in days and weeks I'd be allowed to stay, seemingly indifferent to Daphne's mobile buttocks. The trip also offered an opportunity, away from Lillian, to confess to Daphne that I wasn't as stupid as I was beginning to look. I'd be honest. I was just confused (in my cotton-rich shirt and roomy beige slacks and orangey green running-shoes).

Daphne took a window-seat over the rear wheels, placing her canvas bag carefully between her feet, and I squeezed in next to her as the coach pulled away from the station. She'd made herself up to look older, and she narrowed her disguised, eye-lined eyes. 'Can I trust you?'

'Probably.' Indifference needed more practice. 'I mean you can. Of course you can.'

'It's not too late. You could still turn back.'

'I'll do it. I'm here.' She turned away, and watched through the window the dawn of the town's back-sliding blue-black trees. 'What are we actually doing? We're not going to hurt anybody, are we?'

'Of course not.'

She checked forward and back that no one was looking, then leant down and rummaged inside the bag. I hoped that at last she'd have something to show me which made sense of the trousers.

'Too early,' she said, coming up empty-handed, settling herself back in her seat.

Yesterday, at tea-time, Daphne had told Aunt Lillian we were going to London. She'd said it was my idea. It might even be fun. I also deserved a day off from cartooning, she said, though omitting several other persuasive reasons not connected in any way to the dim-witted dead-end of kissing cousins. She didn't mention, for example, that it was also because I was afraid of being afraid of life, when the alternative to Daphne's raid on London was staying in, avoiding the many terrible things which might otherwise be happening to me.

And if it wasn't me it would have been Roy.

'Good,' Lillian had said, looking at me kindly, half-way through her tea but not really home yet. 'Glad to hear it. About time too.'

She then stood up to open the door, because down near the warehouses to the south of town she'd been counselling the family of a teenager who'd been surfing a red Ford Fiesta. He'd fallen off into the path of an oncoming scaffolding wagon, which had crushed his head like a tin can. As well as the driver, the car was carrying five of his friends. It had all started out as a bit of a laugh.

'We're going by coach,' Daphne had said. 'No need to worry.'

Aunt Lillian had shut the kitchen-door, telling us to take care.

'On second thoughts,' Daphne said, as the bus dipped from a roundabout down to the motorway, 'now's as good a time as any.' She leant forward and reached into the bag, feeling around inside it. She brought out her hand. Flat across the middle-joints of her fingers, draped limply like a single strand of seaweed, was a used yellow condom. A knot was tied in the end to keep it closed.

'Oh Daphne yuck!' Over the headrests I made my own

check forward and back, but no one was watching. 'That is disgusting.'

'Exactly. Imagine finding it where it's not supposed to be.'

She reached inside the bag for more, bringing out a flaccid but colourful handful, like dead eels drawn by children. 'Stop staring. Fill up your pockets.'

Even though they were knotted and audibly dry they felt slimy anyway, slippy and tricky like rubber gloves.

'They're not real, are they? The stuff on the inside.'

'The shock factor's the same whichever.'

'Which means it's all fake, right?'

'Sure. A glob of coconut shampoo, then a knot in the top.'

'You did a great job.' I said. 'I'm genuinely shocked.'

I filled my pockets and wished it was like a comic, and in the next box we simply arrived, made our stand for the swindled classes, kissed like cousins. Not that I was expecting any particular reward, not specifically, at least not beyond finding out how Daphne planned to let it be known that the mischievous small people (which was us) still had minds of our own.

In any case, I suspected I'd be needing my running-away shoes. They were already proving their worth because every time cracks in the road-surface jogged us together I made a check on the thinness of air beneath my feet. But before I could fall we were arriving in London, and browsing through the bus-windows the business of Ladbroke Grove, Marble Arch, Hyde Park, before long losing the view in the vast hangar of Victoria coach station. With our pockets bulging, me with my open-necked shirt and the camera on a camera-strap, Daphne with the canvas bag swinging from her shoulder, we stepped down from our coach like any other newly arrived provincials on that day's ration of the

National Express. Like every other great adventurer, like food.

'First we'll take a good look round,' Daphne said. We were still under cover in the station, awed by the *A–Z*. 'We'll remember the best places and come back to them later. Anywhere smug, airsy and gracey, *London*. But not anywhere too exposed. The little buggers have to stick around long enough to make an impact.'

London that day was covered in cloud, damping the noise of traffic and demolition and reconstruction. Londoners seemed incredibly quick. Either that or they were stopped, under blankets in doorways. I pitied the quick ones. They'd wear themselves thin and commit suicide (all of them, without exception), because the urgency of the capital city had dismantled them, wheels without wagons, fast and light. The clever ones had already stopped, were in retreat, in doorways asking for money for free. They did nothing at all because the intelligent were the first to understand that speed made very little difference.

We took a detour from the line of busy adshels narrowing the pavement, into the enclosed pedestrian thoroughfare of the *Victoria Shopping Centre, Shopping and Eating*. Was this the best that London could offer? It smelt of plastic, and reminded me of America on television. They said that everything which happened over there happened over here ten years later, meaning that London stretched itself thin between the old and the new. It was ancient, but it was also ten years too late.

We crossed several roads to get to Buckingham Palace, and put our faces between the high metal railings. Nothing was happening. We crossed another road and walked uphill in a diagonal across Green Park, to the slapping of striped canvas in the wooden frames of deck-chairs. Birds were

64

singing beneath the cloud cover. Green Park was green. This was just for a moment another Europe, vaguely misremembered, and the sweetness of its slipping-away nearly stopped my heart.

'More brands,' Daphne said, speeding up again at Piccadilly, 'communication for idiots.' Over the restless heads of the guilty she pointed out Exhibition and Shop, Museum and Shop, Hotel and Shop. Otherwise it was just shops, the same but somehow different in famous streets in London. I noticed there weren't many bins. 'Let's go in here,' she said, and I followed her into the *Disney Store* on Regent Street. It was aquarium blue, from ceiling to carpet, like the inside-eye of a soft toy. There was music playing I'd forgotten I remembered, and rows of merchandised characters I recognised without knowing why.

Daphne asked me for some money, and came back from the ringing till with a Mickey Mouse the size of a new-born baby, about as long as my forearm. It was an early smiler. Made in Vietnam.

'Softly softly catchee monkey,' Daphne said, looking pleased with herself. 'It makes us look innocent. And it's also our lucky mascot.'

'How much?'

She told me.

'*How much?*'

She told me again. 'It speaks.'

She pulled a ring attached to a white nylon cord in the middle of the doll's black back. She let it rewind, and in his familiar reedy voice Mickey said: '*Have a Nice Day!*' She pulled it again: '*Gee, Pludo, whaddayasay?*' And again. '*Pow! Right Between the Whiskers!*'

It started to rain, heavy raindrops rebounding from the darkening pavements and the rounded black bonnets of taxis. We took shelter in a *McDonald's*, because they were everywhere, but then Daphne refused to order. I told her she had to order otherwise she wasn't allowed, and while I waited at the counter she balanced Mickey Mouse into a sitting position on a yellow and white table. When I came back, she pulled out the ring and punched the doll on the nose. It fell over sideways.

'Pow! Right Between the Whiskers!'

She wiped off the table with Mickey's ear, and I took a picture. Later, trying to understand what she was like on the inside, I guessed from the photograph that at that precise moment, sheltering in *McDonald's* from the rainy day, wanting someone to blame for just about everything, she blamed *McDonald's*. A few minutes earlier and it would have been the *Disney Store*, and before that Piccadilly, and Buckingham Palace. But in that particular picture she was in *McDonald's*, hating the colours, the lighting, the customers.

She made me notice the staff, who were all about twenty, like in franchises and chains everywhere, the managers present and absent like generals once were, clumsily intrusive until anything went wrong. We watched a sweeping Asian in her cheerful uniform. Daphne said arbeit macht fries.

I said I quite liked the burgers.

'You're nervous, aren't you?' She leant over and sucked at the straw of my strawberry shake. 'Or is it frightened?'

'I'm older than you are. I'm not seeing things quite as clearly.'

She put her hand on mine, warm, smooth, all those lovely slender fingers still intact. She said it wasn't just *McDonald's*. The enemy was everywhere, various but recognisably the same, like members of a street gang. Their names were universally well known: *Nestle*, *Microsoft*, *Nike*, *AOL Time-Warner*, *Coca-Cola*, *Vodafone*, *Sony*, *Glaxo*

66

Wellcome, News International. They were out there controlling the economic policies of our government, but they were also in our houses, and in our clothes, and somewhere up close against our skin. They gave us to eat and to drink. They determined the detail of life, infiltrating ever smaller spaces, and in the future they'd seem such an obvious enemy of the people, like the mafia once were, or the European monarchies, that we'd probably even miss them.

'Something must be done,' Daphne concluded.

'I see. We're going to break the law, aren't we?'

Daphne laughed, then pulled back her hand and did a drum roll on the table with her delicate knuckles. 'As if. Take a look at this.'

She pulled something out of her pocket. Shielding whatever it was with her hand, she leant forward towards me, eyes shining. She let me see it. It was a slim plastic syringe, the needle slightly bent but still attached.

'Bloody hell,' I said. 'That's dangerous.'

It was no use looking her in the eye. Like always, it was a dare. She slid the syringe back across the table, and into one of her pockets.

'You could get that stuck in your leg.' Her tapered leg, varnished in a single brush-stroke from thigh to calf to ankle.

'I'll be careful. I'm wearing a wetsuit.'

I hadn't thought of that. Then I remembered the wrinkled, damp, awkwardly convincing condoms. 'Coconut shampoo. Looks just like the real thing. Right?'

'How strong a stand, exactly, are we planning to make?'

Actually, I hadn't been planning to make any kind of stand at all. Conscience and obstinate resistance were Mum, and everything I wanted to avoid in favour of bullet-proof cartoons, frivolous and straight-edged and applauded. I couldn't cope with Mum's earnestness, and the weight of the world. I wanted to be influenced by the same messages as everyone else, growing younger, inheriting the earth. I knew all about the real world. It was Mum, and it hurt. My pockets suddenly felt very heavy. 'So is it real, or is it fake?'

'It makes no difference.'

'Of course it does.'

'In the bus you agreed it didn't.'

'That's because I wanted it to be fake.'

The fervour was bright in her eyes, the dare and solidity of London, because nothing which happened at home counted as real life. Ask anyone. In that moment, when I could still have backed out, I saw that Daphne was our only hope. Wanting more than anything to grow up, she was acutely sensitive to being treated like a child, burning brightly in the short moment when everything was to be questioned. I drew cartoons; Daphne used all her imagination on life.

'Let's just go and do it,' she said.

'I have to wash my hands.'

'Don't forget the safety-pins.'

A cool wind had blown away the rain and the cloud blushed higher and brighter. It was great soft weather for walking the city, hands in pockets, strolling, sometimes whistling, following Daphne straight back to the *Disney Store* and its disquieting blue eye. 'Here,' she said, behind a rack of medium Snow Whites. The store brought out the wrong kind of child in Daphne, sharp-eyed and wayward, not wide-eyed and passive. As we casually slouched away again, hands innocently in pockets, Mickey safe under Daphne's arm, no-one thought to check for a used condom littering the spot where we'd recently been browsing.

I was supposed to make my drops first, and then take pictures of Daphne. In the excitement she sometimes brushed against me, or like a tourist leant me towards landmarks and London's rightly famous detail. We found a branch of the sunglasses shop. We wandered into household-name supermarkets, museum shops, theme pubs, and the lobby of an international advertising agency. We asked fascinated questions very close to the front-desk of a London local-radio station. Copyrighted, trademarked, these were some among the well-known words we couldn't use freely, and this suddenly seemed another good reason to thin my lips and endure each sheath of cold rubber as it detached itself from my unstitched pocket, and adhered its way down the hairs on my hot bare leg. A wetsuit was a very good idea, but it wasn't one of mine.

Daphne took charge of the targets, more difficult these days than it once was for people like Mum. Back then, the obvious start was us against Vietnam, against South Africa, against ingrained sexism and racism and short-back-and-sides, good (us) hygienically aligned against evil (them). Or perhaps it was only reported that way, after the battles were won. Now we had the same sense of dissatisfaction, but without any emotive photographs of today's starved imaginations to mobilise resistance. Nobody except Daphne knew who to blame: the *Odeon Leicester Square*, the *Chelsea FC* shop at Stamford Bridge, the zebra-crossing in Abbey Road (no access to the *EMI* studios). We went back to *McDonald's*, but a different one, and Daphne simply didn't care: she said their names out loud, despising them for the fun they offered in return.

'In return for what?'

'Everything. Your money and your life. Your soul.'

On the way out of *Segaworld* at the Trocadero I pinched Mickey from under Daphne's arm and pulled his cord. '*Wow Minnie. You Look Swell!*' I was over-excited. I pulled it

69

again. '*Wow Minnie. You Look Swell!*'

Daphne still had her hands cupped in the pockets of her denim dungarees.

'You're finished, then?' Suddenly aware of my free hands, I hid Mickey behind my back. 'All gone.'

'You dropped some two at a time, didn't you?'

'No, not always.'

'Don't get carried away, Danny matey boy. You've still got pictures to take.'

I photographed Daphne in the roped-off queue outside *Planet Hollywood*. I was right behind her, and nearly stood on it, its fake skin pink, moist and milky from the inside out. I stepped over it and waited. Nothing happened. After a while I looked back and took photographs of people avoiding it. A honeymoon couple looked away, deciding this was something on their trip to London they didn't have to believe. The surrounding theme of a movie première was allowed to triumph. A man with a trimmed beard, a Dutchman perhaps, deftly ushered his two young daughters behind him. Pretending to re-buckle his sandal, he reached for the condom with a ball-point pen, and lifted it into his camera bag. I photographed that, too.

Daphne was increasingly mindless about where she made the drops, as if testing everybody else, or testing herself. My cowardly fingers clutched the doll and the camera, and my obedient feet followed her from one dropzone to the next. She thrummed with energy, as if she wasn't one person but many, each one overlapping the other. She flickered, dismissive of the inconvenient distances between London's famous places, finally deciding on a climactic visit to the mother of all parliaments. We walked. I ate a *Snickers*, and held on to the wrapper because London's defining characteristic was its lack of

70

bins. That would explain the condoms to logical tourists. London was so scared of exploding it preferred to fill up with rubbish.

We stepped round outside-broadcast equipment dry under beaded polythene, and with my tongue I worried away at some chocolate burger lodged in the hole in my tooth. Londoners were still fast, and rushing, and I couldn't read any of the faces. They didn't tell stories I could follow, as if the city was suddenly foreign. We slowed behind an electric wheelchair, stood aside for a crocodile of gorgeous children, South Africans or Germans, or just from a private school. But why?

Because they were gorgeous and well behaved, and that's how I understood them from the outside in.

We overtook a very fat woman in a short black skirt and yellow flipflops. Her sunburnt thighs finished below the knee. What did it mean? She was tight inside a strained white tennis-shirt, *the brand of champions*. We avoided a sports boy camouflaged in *Manchester United* from head to toe, one leg lifted as his *Real Madrid* father shouted down at him, their family eyes darting like fish. The language was Russian, or Ukrainian, incomprehensible, black bread, onion-domes. Kalashnikovs. Mercedes. Refugees. Prostitutes. If I hadn't heard them talk, I'd never have known. They were disguised, looking like everyone else in their international brands, as did everyone else.

I felt slow, but not by choice. I didn't understand physical appearance, and couldn't make the connections, not certain where I fitted in or what I was for. Littering London with condoms seemed as muddled, but no more so, than anything else.

Daphne dropped her syringe within sight of a policeman outside the Members entrance to the House of Commons.

71

Instead of taking a photograph, I kicked it against a kerb-stone while Daphne was distracted, whistling and acting the innocent. Nobody saw, and she held up her empty hands, like a jazz singer. She grinned, and for one moment I thought she'd hug me, but instead she snatched Mickey Mouse and aimed him at a passing Londoner, a woman with a leather briefcase, pulling back the string like an arrow.

Pow! Right Between the Whiskers!

'Finished,' Daphne said. 'Bloody brilliant. What next?'

Back to the Trocadero for some ice-rallying in Finland. I didn't dare suggest it. A quiet corner in a pub, where I could write a letter of complaint to my MP. Somewhere romantic, lips up close to the rose of Daphne's delicious ear, a whisper that according to some sources, though admittedly not others, cousins were definitely allowed.

I had no idea what I wanted, or what was the right thing to do. That was more or less the problem.

We crossed the river by Westminster Bridge, using the *A–Z* to get past Waterloo and onto Queen's Walk by the South Bank.

'We should have saved some,' Daphne said, as we strolled downstream past *London Weekend Television*, dodged by cyclists and joggers. She made it harder for them by skipping between the cracks of paving stones, irrepressibly pleased with herself, sometimes looking behind to check we weren't being followed. I think she felt a little cheated by London's security arrangements. Anybody could do anything. It was, however, a minor complaint, because she also sung out lines from songs, and pulled Mickey's cord so many times, aiming him at so many cycling Londoners and innocent tourists, that he eventually jammed on the same phrase, again and again.

Pow! Right Between the Whiskers!

She jumped onto the end of a river-facing bench, scattering a pair of pigeons, holding her arms out wide and walking it like a gymnast's beam. She turned, and I looked into her eyes for guidance, and she was daring me to say it. I sat down near the end of the bench. With the camera I shot from the hip at Daphne at the other end, poised.

'What?' she said.

'Nothing.'

'You wanted to say something.'

'It was nothing. It was silly.'

She shrugged, and stuck one leg straight out. She leant away from the bench, leaning, falling, waiting to overbalance, then jumping at the last moment out and onto the walkway. She went and put her elbows on the parapet overlooking the river, her chin in her hands, gazing at the spreading wake of a pleasure-boat.

'Somebody had to do something,' she said. I joined her at the parapet, both of us staring down at the slow brown river.

'Not necessarily me, though.' I watched a tired dredger grump upstream. 'I'm supposed to be drawing cartoons.'

Daphne gave in to one of her boxed sterling-silver laughs. She pushed herself away from the parapet and jumped back onto the bench. She spread out her arms, looming above me. 'It was fun, though, wasn't it?'

I scrunched up my eyes and beamed my teeth, like I'd practised in the mirror. 'Whoop-whoop,' I said.

This wasn't what I'd had in mind. Individuals had no business squaring up to corporate giants. You didn't have to be a genius to work out the comical mismatch, the cartoon special. I didn't want to get involved. I'd had a bang on the head, the better to appreciate the smooth the up the swings, not the rough the down the roundabouts.

73

I should have told her that dissent was something I'd already tried, when I was younger. It wasn't much fun in the end. During a year at Art School, open and closed, stopping and starting, I'd tried some of the many things I wasn't officially allowed. I'd accepted every drug offered, for example, but never bought my own, meaning I experimented with most substances once. Then there was my phase with Mum, learning that nobody could be clever and happy without making a stand. It was the third possible combination, along with stupid and conformist, or clever and miserable.

'Poor Daniel. I'll tell you what. You've done something for me. I'll do something for you. Your idea of fun, anything, you name it.'

Her eyes. I tried them again and was suddenly flustered by the possibility of her thinking what I was thinking, with the same bedroom illustrations. Her discarded black polo-neck and knickers. Distracting myself, I went back to the bench, desperately trying to think of something allowed and safe and plausibly fun for all the family. 'Let's try something fun which doesn't break the law.'

'We could go drinking.'

'Tried it.' But stopped again when the morning-after began to frighten me with its peep-shows of forgotten mistakes, vivid but fixed and in two flat dimensions. 'Besides, you're only sixteen.'

She sat beside me, batted her eyelids, crossed her legs, took one of my hands inside two of hers. We were like a couple of old people, an old couple. 'You name it,' she said, and I was more convinced than ever that it was preferable to learn through pleasure (cartoons) than pain (complications).

'Actually,' I said. 'There is somewhere. I've wanted to go there from the moment I banged my head.'

'Wherever. I'll do whatever you want.'

'You have to promise to behave.'

'Promise.'

'Seriously.'

'Cross my heart and hope to die. Where are we going?'

'A place where fun's guaranteed. It's like a cathedral exclusively devoted to fun. Everyone says it's magic.'

'Sounds expensive,' Daphne said. 'Are you sure that's what you want?'

'It's our best chance. Sixty million paying customers can't all be wrong.'

Draw an hourglass, flat at top and bottom.
Insert V neckline and slope the shoulders.
Indicate the collar-bone, and shape the breasts, to
taste.

Elbows level with the indent of the waist.
The heavier the body, the wider the legs.
Arch the feet and tip the toes. Experiment.
As one shoulder dips, the hip on the same side rises.

Move her about. Walk her, run her, jump her round
the frame-sheet.
You can't hurt her. She's all surface.

The face is an oval, divided by fractions, eyes, nose,
mouth.
The neck is a cylinder in measurable proportion.
She can't hurt you back, either.

Frank Babbitt's room on the second floor of the *Yurayama* staff-accommodation block had a matching self-assembly table and chair, and a narrow door to a bathroom unit with shower. One eye open, sprawled on his stomach in bed, Frank could see his personal armchair, and the shelves above it he'd installed himself. He was home sweet home.

The day was already bright behind the single roll-up blind. His head. He should have been at work hours ago. Last night, Paris, Jeanne of the emptiable dress.

He wished he hadn't drunk so much. That would be to blame for making him drunk. He climbed out of bed, and conquered his headache long enough to call the attractive voice at Personnel, with how weak he was feeling, and ill, and at least for the rest of the day. Hers was a voice with curves in it, and frankly disbelieving eyebrows. Sick, very very sick, Frank insisted, and yes he fully understood the implications for the Christmas Golden Beak awards.

Soon, he'd take a shower, but first of all the armchair. He pulled on some jogging pants, and a white round-necked sweater. He was going to collapse into the chair and sit there doing nothing, and he wasn't going to smile while he was doing it. He collapsed into the chair.

Someone knocked at the door.

'Go away.'

'It's me.'

'Who's me?'

Guess: Frank scrabbles to escape along the floor of a canyon. A falling fridge lands dangerously close. Following right behind it, by parachute, stretching from his pocket a full-size sweeper's shovel, the pursuer in this cartoon pursuit lands and steps out calmly from behind a cactus. And CLANG! He whacks the fleeing Frank Babbitt clean in the moving midriff. Oof! Frank woozes and wobbles and then walls over.

'It's me, Michael Miller.'

'You're not supposed to come here.' Frank didn't move from his chair. He raised his voice at the closed door. 'You should be at work.'

'It's my lunch-break. There's been an incident.'

Frank sighed, and went to open the door. Michael had changed into casuals, his jeans and a pink sweatshirt with a printed transfer of the sexy heroine character from *Oedipus Rex*.

'I'm off-duty,' Frank said, blocking the doorway. 'It's not my problem.'

'I found this.'

Michael held up a slim syringe with a bent needle. He'd found it next to a model of Big Ben in *The Swinging Sixties*, and without having to be told he'd discreetly swept it into his musketeer's dustpan. He didn't think anyone else had seen.

'So what's new?' Frank said. 'Sometimes they even drop used rubbers.'

Michael was amazed, outraged. 'Who does? Why?'

Frank grimaced. He rubbed the web of skin between thumb and forefinger over the unchecked stubble on his chin. He considered one of the many possible answers, polished it, held it up to the light.

'They want to get us bad publicity,' he explained, wearily massaging the heels of his hands against his temples. 'Maybe

80

even a court-case. They don't like us. They're a little con-fused.'

'If only I could catch them red-handed.'

Frank put a lid on the bubbling duck, and told Michael it was about time he was getting back.

'I also have a complaint.' Michael's expression was grim, determined. He concentrated hard on the door-frame, and picked at a paint-blister with his real-life fingernails. 'You abandoned me in Paris.'

What was Frank supposed to say? 'Life is unfair, Michael.' There, all said and done. You can go now.

'I didn't get back until after midnight. Some of the others were having a party. They threw me in the lake.'

'Alas. Human nature.'

'Fully clothed. You made me a promise, Frank.'

'I'm a very small cog.'

Michael's flesh and quick fingers, nails bitten to the blood, played a studied exercise for piano on the wood of the door-frame. He was close to tears, and only Frank could save him, the same Frank who should have noticed by now that such unnatural dedication deserved its reward. Frank stepped back from the doorway. Michael stepped forward. Surprised, Frank stepped back again, and to Michael this was clearly an invitation. He went all the way in, grateful, thrilled, composing himself by the bookshelf in a feigned assessment of Frank's many paperbacks.

'What do you want, Michael?'

Michael scanned the spines, put a finger to his lips. 'Just think,' he said, tears almost dry, 'if you hadn't spent so much time reading.'

I could have been a surfer, Frank thought. An actor, a contented theme-park employee.

'What happens in this one?' Michael pulled out a book,

satisfied now that quite properly everything was turning out well. The book was *Crime and Punishment*. 'What's this one all about, then, Frank?'

Frank felt tired, hungover and turning nasty. That one? The hero a handsome student wins a soldier's daughter with some jewels he steals from a mean old crone. After some comic dealings with bungling policemen, they live happily ever after.

'Strange,' Michael said, taking a second look at the cover. 'I heard it was more depressing than that.'

From beneath the self-assembly table he pulled out Frank's matching, straight-backed chair. He sat on it backwards, facing into the room. Frank was scandalised, enraged, furious with himself for having spoken and letting Michael speak back, like a conversation. 'Tell me what you want, Michael. Then you better go.'

'Make me a character.'

'Why? All the other staff pick on you. They ganged up and threw you in the lake. Why do you think they did that?'

'Because I have a hand and a leg missing, and funny eyes.'

'No, Michael, that's not why. It's because you take the park far too seriously. That really pisses them off. You have no sense of humour. That's because you have no sense of reality either, to compare it with.'

'I do.'

'What are your parents' names?'

'That's irrelevant.'

'What is your father's first name, Michael?'

'I don't have a real father. The man who called himself my father treated me badly because he didn't love me. The reason being that he wasn't really my father.'

'What was his name?'

'A master-craftsman woodworker applied to adopt me.'

Frank laughed. He knew Michael was trying to impress, and the laughter must have hurt, but Frank didn't care. It was kinder to do it like this than to scoff and heave him into the lake, again and again.

'What happened to your leg, Michael?'

'You promised.'

'What happened to your hand? Tell me what really happened and I'll do what I can.'

Michael's eyes coincided perfectly, like they had in the bar in Paris when he was crushing Frank's fingers. Frank settled himself in the armchair, facing Michael, ready to listen. Michael made up his mind.

'My father's name is Dennis,' he said. He gripped the back of the chair, blew out his cheeks. 'My mother's name is Joan. They live in Oldham in the north of England, where they look after my collection. I'm an only child, so they have plenty of time.'

'What happened to your hand?'

'I lost it in a waste-disposal incident at the kitchen sink.'

'Fuck.'

'I didn't expect it to hurt so much.'

'What?'

'I went ballistic. Dad bought me a wind-up post-war Felix at auction.'

'You put your own hand down the waste-disposal unit?'

'There was a 1937 Betty Boop. Mint. That's what I asked for, but he never listens.'

'I don't believe it,' Frank said. He started to see the sense of it. He'd always known what kind of person expected every dream to come true. 'You're a spoilt child. Who paid for your arm and your leg?'

'It was the least they could do. I wanted to be a character, so I had to have the best. Now can I be Cocky Chicken?'

83

'What happened to your leg?'

'You said I could be Cocky. I've told you the truth.'

'What happened to your leg?'

'You promised, Frank.'

'The leg, Michael.'

'You're not going to help me, are you?'

'Tell me about your leg.'

Michael held his breath. Veins hardened in his neck and started to tremble. 'It was outside great-uncle Neptune's underwater palace,' he exploded, breathing in and out, twice, three times. 'My leg was eaten in a sandwich by the propeller of a singing steamboat.'

'Also,' Frank added calmly, 'you forgot to tell me about your mother.' Now he was just being cruel, and not even to be kind. Michael shoved away his chair. It slapped diagonally against the bathroom door, rolled its shoulders, fell. Not enough. He turned and wiped all Frank's papers off the table, making several sweeps with his unfeeling plastic hand. 'My mother was shot in the forest, and that's a fact.'

Michael's voice was louder, less controlled, but Frank couldn't help himself. 'Then what, Michael? Tell me about this forest. Who was it who shot her?' Frank was trapped in the armchair, licking his lips, fascinated by how far they were both prepared to go. 'Then what, Michael?'

'Then I joined the circus, but my ears were too big.' He clenched his fists, and looked for something to break. He was nearly crying again. 'My mother was locked in a wagon. My evil stepmother is trying to kill me. She wants my heart in a box.'

'Don't hit me, Michael.'

'No pain! No pain! No pain!'

He smashed his fake hand against the spines of the books just above Frank's head. Frank ducked and raised his arms, his feet lifting off the floor, finding out exactly how far they were both prepared to go. He was about to die in his own room because Michael Miller wanted light entertainment to sustain him. Michael stepped back and started singing. He conducted himself with wild swings of his arms.

'I'VE GOT NO STRINGS TO TIE ME DOWN!'

He stopped singing. No more conducting. He told Frank he'd be a character, just you wait and see, then reached for the door-handle and stumbled into the corridor. 'HI HO! HI HO!', and to every HO! he slammed his plastic hand against a solid surface, never quite reaching the words of the song.

In a whisper, Frank helped him out. *It's off to work we go.*

He pushed himself right to the back of the armchair, and the books dislodged by Michael dropped in a clump from the shelves. They landed heavily on Frank's head. He covered his stinging ears and folded his body sideways, his undirected gaze snagging on the turned-up legs of the chair. Frank had been cruel, and once upon a time he'd cared about such things. Now, he failed to rouse any great nostalgia for his better self. He resented his youthful idealism, and the foolish dream of exquisite European melancholy.

Sheets of paper and splayed paperbacks were spread across the carpet, and Frank seemed to remember from his book-reading that he'd once had a soul. Yes, he had one of those. He must have, to feel so unhappy, and his disastrous career in a theme-park was evidence enough that the soul or spirit doesn't just break, like a breaking heart. The soul shrinks and wastes away. Like a muscle, it needs to be useful, and used.

My life had been stuck again, and it had needed starting again, and in the end I had a history of submitting to the popular pressure to follow a story. I had to be a character, and making an episode of a trip to *Disneyland Paris* was a way of postponing the terrifying white space between episodes. Me.

It also felt like a last chance. I was optimistic that life could be good and people could change. I didn't have to be like Mum, clever but only happy when doing what we weren't allowed. I could be like the adults illustrating the brochures I'd picked up at the travel agency. *Amazed, awe-struck, surprised, thrilled, and always, always, ecstatically happy*. It seemed unlikely, but just maybe it was possible, otherwise why would they say it?

The evening before we were due to leave, at tea-time, Lillian quizzed us about London.

'This time we're going right over London's head,' Daphne said, avoiding the question. 'We're getting our fun from source.'

Aunt Lillian beamed, because this was her second major breakthrough in a single day. At last, tea-time was working – Daphne had stopped sulking. More impressively, Lillian could see as I could that Daphne was genuinely excited about tomorrow's trip to *Disneyland Paris*. Just as she'd hoped, my stay in the spare room had eventually turned out well, because I was younger, and I wasn't Daphne's mother, and therefore she'd listened to me. Aunt Lillian liked the idea that from now on Daphne would be getting on well with the world, and everything in it.

After London, I was less easily persuaded by Daphne's good-girl transformation, but Aunt Lillian's optimism was infectious. Also, Daphne had promised to behave, vowing to take *Disneyland Paris* as it came, on its merits, as an outing, a break, a fun day-out for the child hide-and-seeking in us all. If she actually enjoyed herself, which Lillian and I both secretly expected, then she'd have to admit that she wasn't exceptional. She hadn't been dropped into the cauldron as a baby, nor been genetically muddled with an insect. She'd missed out on one of those fortunate upbringings ominously close to illegal radioactive vats.

She too would have to accept the eternal mismatch of us against them. It was an unfair contest, and therefore shouldn't happen, and as this is what I wanted to believe, I believed it. Daphne was sixteen, and I was a novice cartoonist. We hadn't the public standing to accuse and attack the foundations of this recreational century.

In fact, that evening before we left, we were so excited we acted like a happy family, chattily volunteering our respective previous encounters with Disney. Apart from the word itself, which was everywhere and unavoidable, and some of the early cartoon films, Daphne claimed she knew hardly anything.

'Go on,' I said, wanting her to be honest, to behave herself. 'Everyone's had more contact than that.'

She'd heard somewhere that before he died, Walt Disney had arranged for his corpse to be frozen until such time as the technology was invented to revive it.

My own previous experience, not counting inevitable exposure to the tableware and toothbrushes, and I remember now a Christmas pair of boxer shorts, and my most recent box of cereals, occasional hotel afternoons with *The Disney Channel*, a recent Radio 5 Live report on the possible Disney purchase of *Newcastle United Football Club*, and our brief double-visit to the *Disney Store* in London's Regent Street, well apart from all that (and knowing the name Michael Eisner), apart from that, my only feature-length exposure to the Walt Disney Company was in Berlin with those two animated films, *The Little Mermaid* and *Hercules*.

Also, I didn't think it was Walt's whole body; I'd read somewhere they'd only frozen his head.

Lillian was the surprise winner. She'd actually been there, to the original *Disneyland* theme-park, in Anaheim, California.

'We went as children. Yes Daniel, your Mum too.'

Aunt Lillian, with her daily experience of the real world, said that every home she went into had its own Disney story, so we shouldn't be surprised that she also had hers. She went to open the door to the yard, out of habit, but then remembered it wasn't that kind of story.

Of course in her day it had been much less intense (before home video and public relations and the European park), and mostly it had meant stopping all other games late on Saturday afternoon for *The Wonderful World of Disney*, on BBC 1. In amongst the cartoon clips they always broadcast a report from the California theme-park, which used to look artificial because the characters were much more convincing as cartoons.

At Aunt Lillian's school, way back when (before the *Disney Stores* and tie-ins with *McDonald's* paper-cups, before *McDonald's*), her whole class had wanted to go to America and go (they all watched late-afternoon BBC, on

Saturday). Aunt Lillian and Mum turned out to be the lucky ones, *Pan-Am*, a grand family holiday, a children's amusement-park making the two girls directly responsible for general collective happiness and value for money. It had been great, but. They both told their parents many many times how fantastic it all was.

'It was fine,' Lillian said, 'but *The Wonderful World of Disney* had led us to expect something better. Something utterly fantastic. Unreal, almost.'

Back at home, disenchanted, my own mother began to recognise other false promises, too much for too little. She learnt how to be angry at the era's casually traded deceptions, its pattern of raised expectations falling flat. Aunt Lillian reacted differently, devoting all her energy to what she perceived as reality. Unlike her disillusioned sister, most people in the real world weren't taking a stand. Earning a living, bringing up Daphne, restraining herself, Aunt Lillian kept both feet firmly on the ground.

'Well,' I said, 'I never knew that.' Or maybe I did know that, but the more I forgot the simpler it became.

Daphne found it equally amazing. 'So it was Disney which first set off Daniel's Mum?'

'Probably not only that,' Lillian said, 'and like always she went too far. Still does.'

'And anyway,' I said, 'it's different now.'

Aunt Lillian was flicking through the brochures. 'My visit was thirty years ago,' she said. 'It doesn't have any bearing.'

In general terms, the holiday guides gave us a good idea of what to expect. *Disneyland Paris* was a carefully regulated experience of objects and adventures which looked real but weren't. That's what made it fun, exactly because it wasn't real, or true, which in a small but nagging way was a pity. It meant that pleasure and pretending went together, giving pain the benefit of being the only real thing, like a bad day at Lillian's office.

In a lay-by on the bypass to the east of town, a lorry-driver had picked up a young French girl, hitching. He'd raped her, killed her, then kept the corpse for several weeks in the sleeping compartment at the back of his cab. Later, defending himself in court, he'd sworn on oath that she'd wanted it. He'd described to the jury in some detail how she'd loved every minute of it.

Lillian told us to be careful out there. 'Oh heavens to buggery,' she added, jumping up, 'the door!' She opened it anyway, even though it was too late.

Very early the next morning, on our regular coach service to London, sitting over the wheels, I wore pale-blue shorts with a brown leather belt, and black socks with my running-shoes. Just like the last time, this was the National Express, and in the next box we didn't simply arrive. Daphne either looked out at the motorway, or talked about socks.

Most people were trying to be clever, she said, or cool. This usually meant pretending they knew something which other people didn't. When they didn't. Which meant in actual fact they were being stupid. Cool was therefore basically stupid. Uncool was the new cool, and always had been, which was why she liked my socks.

She seemed preoccupied. Her mind was unpredictable as an animator's cat, sometimes straight and logical, then twisted like a rubber-band. On the one hand, she told me that Disney wanted to colonise fantasy and memory through carefully controlled and widely disseminated images. On the other, touching my thigh, she said she hoped we didn't miss Mickey.

She'd chosen her London dungarees and *Save the Tiger*, which made me worry. In honour of our special day I wanted to believe she'd suspended her basic reforming principle that something had to be done, and at this stage I was glad she seemed uncharacteristically subdued. It was as if she was determined to keep her promise. No doubt she'd liven up once we actually arrived, *a marvel-a-minute around every corner*. No beggars, no unhappiness, no predatory males. I imagined she was quietly coming to terms with the many advantages.

On the Underground between Victoria and Waterloo, changing at Embankment, she successfully ignored the capital's provocation. I again toyed with the idea of confessing I wasn't as stupid as I looked, but thought it sounded stupid. And I wasn't sure I believed it anymore.

As she jolted against me, not minding the gap, I had to stick strictly to the chalked skin at the rippled point of her elbow. When she smiled, it was the glisten on her new white teeth. Like two short planks, I'd left it open as to whether and where we were staying the night, and only a half-wit would have prolonged this infantile crush on a teenage cousin. I mean would have been tempted to think of living it out, instead of just dreaming it.

'Are you sure you've got enough money?' Lillian had asked.

I had, even though it was supposedly earmarked for cartoon-time. We bounced shoulders on the tube, upper arms, elbows. It wasn't as if I hadn't had other girlfriends, on and off, while Mum was selecting bandannas, designing placards, organising demonstrations. My first girlfriend,

Vicky, wore a bandanna and designed placards. My second girlfriend, Janet, organised demonstrations and wore a bandanna. A pattern seemed about to emerge, but both these episodes were doomed because the girls refused the model of a three-act structure learnt from films, wanting it more than anything, suffering a setback, struggling on to soft fulfilment and an unchallenged ending.

If you didn't try for it, it couldn't happen. I hardly needed a bang on the head because I'd been acting stupidly *all the bloody time*. Then as now it would have made much more sense to aspire to a stolidly traditional type of daydream, aiming among other essentials for the regular hand-in-hand. Smiling, sometimes singing, I and my most dearly, we'd live happily from one day to the next, the familiar endings still what most of us were obstinately after.

At Waterloo, I saw many more of those stopped Londoners in doorways and under blankets, making it a relief to click through into the separate section for *Eurostar*, another of life's many protected areas which needed a ticket. On a steel and red-leather seat, waiting for the train, we were predictably besieged by billboard adverts promising the usual happy endings, sex and respect and holidays, with some whoop-whoop fun for the journey.

We hardly noticed. These and similar images had always been our everyday background, so no wonder that was the kind of happiness we wanted. After so many promises we assumed the beachy Disney horizons as a right, not the brick walls of tricky British business addresses into Euro *Yellow Pages*. Daphne had never had to do that. She still hadn't realised that false promises were endlessly preferable.

It was a choice, like the Disney version of *Hercules*.

Either the hero lived happily ever after, or in agony he burnt to death, but only one of these versions projected the map of what was actually out there. Europe was old, and sick, and in its important stories something else was usually waiting to happen after the happy ending, a habit of pessimism learnt from history. *Come dream with your eyes wide open.*

'It's going to work,' I said, determined to think wish-fulfilment, knowing which of the two maps I'd prefer to live. There was *Space Mountain* and *Phantom Manor. Beware, tricks and pranks are the name of the game!* 'Just you wait and see. When they get it right it's like in the adverts. Entertainment and consumption can be forces for liberation.'

'From what?'

'Anxiety.'

'Who's anxious?'

Space Mountain bombards your senses. Risk it if you dare!

I said: 'Let yourself go.'

The *Eurostar* was timetabled London to *Disneyland Paris* without changes, a straight line of communication between Europe's eminent centres. On the train, while the garden of England was still green, I saw a column of rain trapped in sunlight, in the distance over the fields towards the coast. I wished the train would hurry up, and move a little faster past half-timbered oast-houses and the golf-courses. I wanted to get there. *Speed your way to the heart of the magic.* The tunnel sucked us in, darkness before France, and then the fields of Normandy interminable and flat like a pre-Disney holiday.

For Daphne's benefit I breezily described, reading from the brochure, how in *Disneyland Paris* you could change your appearance on a computer screen. *Stretch your nose, enlarge your ears, grow long hair, or make your eyes bigger than your belly!* But the longer we spent on the train, and the more excited the faces around us became, the more subdued Daphne seemed, unlike I'd ever seen her. I nudged her with my elbow, and playfully challenged her to tell me something true, anything, while she still had the chance. 'Go on,' I said. 'It won't bite.'

'Coconut shampoo,' she said, hugging tight the talking Mickey Mouse. It was still our lucky mascot, and luckily, we didn't have to bother too much with France. It provided the pretty pictures in the train's high-speed window while we bought coffee from the trolley in English. *The beating of the tom-toms is a warning of your coming!*, I read, *But beware, you're in pirate territory!* The train may have stopped, once or perhaps even twice, but we never had to leave our seats. *It's everything you always dreamt of!*

Towards the end of the line, I stood and stretched as eagerly as anyone, passing down Daphne's canvas bag from the overhead rack. The train slowed, and we queued along the aisle. It stopped, and we filed onto the platform, knowing everyone else had the same sensational destination. There were good-looking young people out in force to welcome us. They showed us the way, up the escalators and out of the rail terminal, winding along the well-swept *Promenade Disney* of engraved rose-granite hexagons.

The Cousins Travers. 21st Century.

And then we were there. That was it, more or less, how in next to no time, like anyone with enough money who fancied it for whatever reason, the two of us, Daphne and me, English cousins, dressed down for the bright midsummer sunshine, carrying between us a small canvas bag and a

94

talking Mickey Mouse doll, came to be standing dwarfed in the barred shadow of the immense forest-green gates of the legendary *Disneyland Paris*.

Which is where I have to stop.

TWO

I've remembered one of the many things I'm not allowed to do.

I'm not allowed to tell my own story in *Disneyland Paris*. It's like taking in your own lunch.

At the beginning, I set out with no other notion than the simple quest for some harmless fun. It's an amusement-park, for children, and I just wanted to tell the story of me and Daphne in a recognisable public place, open to anyone who can afford the entrance. Mickey and Minnie in their park of attractions on God's green earth exist in our common culture. They're part of the way we explain our time to ourselves.

Personally, I harboured no grudge. However, I've since learnt of many others who do. The nine hundred and forty staff, for example, dismissed without warning from *Eurodisney* before the routinely expensive Christmas of 1993 (all those merchandised mark-ups!). The Walt Disney Company was sorry, of course it was, but even in the Magic Kingdom redundancies were an economic reality. I heard of troublemakers with even longer memories who still bristled at Walt Disney's false denunciation of rival cartoonists as communists. And other grumblers again were often calling for a belated stand to be made for women, or Jews, or blacks, or simply all the non-unionised employees unprotected then as now. I was never one of these people.

Nor could I count myself among the livid artistic purists like the Hugo family, of Victor Hugo fame. Five great-grandchildren of the great novelist had famously sent an open letter to the President of the French Republic, accusing the Walt Disney Company of cultural plunder and artistic simplification. They reviled Disney for avoiding pain, and alienation, and ambiguity, to name only three of the more authentic amusements of contemporary life in Europe. The Hugos complained that their grandfather's landmark novel, *Notre-Dame de Paris – 1482*, had been pillaged and disfigured, twisted into the exploitative format of a Disney cartoon. They urged the European peoples to resist now, before it was too late, because it didn't stop at cartoon versions of classic novels. They contested that the Disney Company systematically polluted everything it touched.

I don't claim to have had an opinion. All I wanted was to tell my story.

Only I now discover that my version of a straight story in this Disney-owned part of the known world is disallowed. *The Happiest Place on Earth*. Copyrighted, trademarked, withdrawn in the untouchable name of trade. I'm not allowed to reproduce their language, nor any images from inside the park. That's the law. It's a brick wall, and there's no getting past it, not even in cartoons, which therefore fail early at Walt's ideal of *everything the mind of man can conceive*.

During this unexpected but enforced white space, I should also state that Frank Babbitt and Michael Miller are entirely imaginary, and bear no relation to any real person, living or dead.

Having said that, it's always possible that characters like Frank and Michael genuinely exist in *Disneyland Paris*, but if so they're living under assumed names. Equally, there might be two amusement-park staff in quite another amusement-park, like *Yurayama*, with coincidentally the *same* two names. It's a small world, after all.

And anyway, most of the interesting stuff between Frank and Michael happened in Paris, the great European city. Everything inside *Yurayama* was necessarily tame. It was limited to what's allowed, and the truth is that from beginning to end I'd have liked this story to take place in *Disneyland*. I could have written it, too, if only my optimism had been justified, and we'd loved every minute of it. *Stunning in every detail, no matter what age you are, every moment here is magic!*

That way, I'd have been allowed. It would have been easier, too. Easier to play dumb, and nothing matters, and recognise the world as they've trademark-registered to have it recognised. *It's as Big as Imagination Itself*. Follow their itinerary, in their interests. Tell their kind of story, or the kind they're happy for us to hear. Use their culture of captured words to describe a limited, self-interested, privately controlled version of the way we are, impervious, even hostile to different ways of seeing.

But Daphne saw things differently, which left us stranded at the gates of the park, where I learnt that the world we actually live in is frequently forbidden as background. What this means is that before long all non-corporate stories will have to take place exclusively in unrecognisable places. As realism is gradually disallowed, by law, then stories other than theirs begin to distort, and sound like they never happened.

Yurayama, my arse. *Cocky Chicken*, my arse. This is a true story.

Imagine *Main Street USA* beside a plundered Aztec temple just beyond the Paris ring-road. The imaginative challenge of Cocky and Clucky as great big-headed replacements and fakes is no more difficult than that.

As it happened then, and in real time, after discussions with lawyers and many months of careful consideration, I came to the conclusion that we never once stepped through the gates of the theme-park *Disneyland Paris*. Daphne and I didn't set foot together inside trademark-protected property at any time.

On that fateful summer day we both stood, excited for different reasons, in the gaps between the bars in the shadow of the gates of the park. We didn't need to live locally to *Main Street USA* to know where we were. It made a reliable impression, as instantly recognisable as the Taj Mahal or Downing Street, but as we peered through the gates it was made strange after all by its unfamiliar reality. We'd eventually made it, and here it was, and the leaves of trees on the other side were the same mottled green as leaves in our English gardens. Stone looked cold to the touch. Above us the broken, dozing cloud moved just like cloud. Fortunately, gazing from the outside in, not everything was the same. There was a vague sense of modern items missing, like traffic and overhead power-lines, and here it was always a holiday, and Handel's *Messiah* for ensemble triangle, and each bright facade of *Main Street* coloured-in one coloured crayon at a time.

An antique fire-engine, red from a brand-new tube, ringing its bell. A uniformed railroad porter, a century out of date, cheerfully sweeping spent cigarettes into a dustpan on a stick. A toothy dog, tall and restless in an overtight waistcoat and a soft, animated hat. A brown bear in spectacles jigging with children. So many anomalies, so little time.

It was Daphne's fault that we didn't get any further. In those skinned trainers and London dungarees and that loose-necked *Save the Tiger*, she might just as well have added a bandanna. What a brainless dope I must have been to think she'd change overnight. Just before the turnstiles, money out to buy the tickets, she came back to life. She tried to get in half-price.

'Are you under the age of twelve?' From inside the narrow kiosk a ticket-girl smiled brightly. No make-up. No aviator-style glasses. A pill-box hat, and a distinctly positive outlook. She was pretty, too.

'Not exactly, no,' Daphne said, hands sulking deep in her denim pockets, shoulders high, pushing out her lower lip. 'But I'm buying a ticket for the child Disney brings out in us all.'

I pulled her away, but she was already shouting that this was a legitimate protest against adult prices in a children's amusement-park starting at the age of twelve. *Cynics! Exploiters of children!*

We found ourselves tumbled back outside in no time, coughing through rising clouds of see-through dust. I personally landed on my head, because my hands were occupied with the Mickey Mouse doll, but then a forward roll brought me into a sitting position side-by-side with Daphne, our legs veed out in front of us, like children. 'And don't come back!' they might just as well have said, cleaning their hands of the dust of us by slicing them together like cymbals.

'Now look what you've done.'

We felt banned for life, and that's when we should have gone home. Daphne put a consoling arm round my shoulders.

'Poor Daniel. Poor Danny-boy. I've ruined your day, haven't I?'

'You promised not to make any trouble. It was supposed to be fun.'

'Daniel, Daniello, it's probably for the best.'

'Now we'll never know.'

'I've been keeping a secret.'

103

She took her bag off her shoulder and placed it between her knees. She pulled out all three pens of my magic-marker set. She did high eyebrows, constructing an apology out of open hands and a wide thin mouth.

'That's not all,' she said, dropping the pens back in the bag. From her right-hand dungaree pocket she took out a translucent knotted condom, and swung it like a watch. She blew out her upper lip and rolled her eyes, briefly hunching her shoulders. From her other pocket she pulled out a dried used tampon.

'Oh, Daphne.'

'Tomato ketchup.' She put it back in her pocket. 'I was going to tell you, honestly. Too late now, anyway.'

'I'm not really stupid.'

'Of course you aren't.' She squeezed my shoulder and shook the magic markers and the condom and the tampon to the bottom of the bag.

'Daphne, listen. I never had a nasty bang on the head. It's all a big act.'

'Sure.' She buckled the bag closed and stood up and hung it from her shoulder.

'I've had other lives. I've been to other places. I'm not as slow as I look.'

'I know. You just said.' She twisted round and slapped dust from the backs of her legs. 'But thinking you're not stupid is usually the best proof that actually you are.'

'Sorry?'

'Exactly. If you were so clever you'd understand.'

'I never said I was clever, just that I wasn't slow.'

'Give me an example, then,' she said.

She was up. I was still down. I bit hard on one of Mickey's ears. Then, there on my bum in the dust and gravel, the gates of *Disneyland Paris* looming behind us, I made my first truly stupid mistake. I said I knew of somewhere we could stay in the centre of Paris, with a man called Chang Chung-Jen, a friend of my mother's from the anti-everything days, in the past best forgotten, air-brushed, unstudied.

I told Daphne that Chang Chung-Jen was a veteran of the Vietnam war, because I wanted to impress her, and because I was stupid. However, I'd forgotten how famously difficult it was to guess anything about him from the outside, especially if he refused to speak.

That evening he agreed to meet us in his upstairs flat, some distance beyond the Eiffel Tower, where at the far end of a spacious room we found him sitting poised like an actor, on a polished wooden chair with the high-backed style of a throne. His feet and knees he kept pressed together, resting his hands lightly palm-down on his thighs. He wore a high-necked tunic, in green silk, with black cotton trousers and yellow espadrilles, and he'd hardly changed at all except for being older. His greying hair fell in a diagonal sweep across his forehead, and his unblinking eyes were dark and slippery like carbon graphite. The rest of his face was almost feminine, fine-boned and cruel, an impression strengthened by his pursed cherry-red lipstick.

Impassively, inscrutably, he lifted up his delicately clenched fist. I did the same.

'Us against them,' I said. Daphne looked at me with her mouth open.

Then she turned back to Chang and introduced herself. 'I'm Daphne. Pleased to meet you.' She raised her fist. 'Us against them.'

Chang bowed his head, briefly closing his eyes, meaning

for us to sit on the two low stools arranged to face him. Then he bowed his head a second time, and a slender Asiatic girl, in lopsided sunglasses and a traditional split-sided dress, came in carrying a tea-pot. On a low table she set out bowls decorated with dragons, and pushed aside a casual gun. Another gun. We'd all seen hundreds of the things, thousands. They were such predictable unreal objects, common as shoes, banal as cups of tea, but I think we were still immensely impressed by an actual gun. Daphne sat on her hands, and lifted her feet off the floor. Chang took a delicate sip from his enamelled bowl, then froze, the tea at his lips, staring with exaggerated eyes at the Mickey Mouse face-down across my knees.

He put down his bowl and visibly composed himself, his face closing again and setting hard. His hands once more came to rest lightly on his thighs.

'We didn't go in or anything,' Daphne said. 'We were thrown out. It was all over in seconds.'

'Just a bit of fun,' I said, avoiding Chang's cold eyes by turning Mickey over and sitting him up. Respectfully, I bobbed his head at Daphne, then Chang. 'It doesn't mean anything.' Mickey nodded, seriously agreeing it meant nothing at all.

'Don't mind Daniel,' Daphne said, dropping her voice. 'He's sometimes a bit slow.'

'It's a children's amusement-park,' I said, letting go of Mickey. He toppled off my knees, and onto the floor. I looked at him, then left him. 'There's nothing wrong with it. It has cute cartoon characters which small children quite like.'

Chang had me flustered. I remembered him as someone it was difficult to take seriously, a faded cabaret performer useful to the revolution in a supporting role, often involving

107

hammy acting and confidence tricks. But in that first instant after seeing the Mickey Mouse, Chang's face had betrayed a pure and intense hatred. It hadn't lasted long, but long enough for me to know that however much that look had cost, and however much it hurt, I didn't want to pay or to suffer that much.

He snapped his elegant fingers. The Asiatic girl knelt down beside him, and lowered her head. She never smiled. He stroked her tied-back hair, and then adjusted the frames of her black-lensed glasses, setting them straight on her nose. She reached out for his tea but he stopped her with a click of his tongue. She knelt up straight, her back in an interrupted line with her thighs. He whispered something in her ear, his lips hidden behind her head. It sounded like Chinese, or French.

'He say, call me Wendy,' the girl said, her head still, the heavy sunglasses hiding wherever it was she was looking. Then Chang whispered into her ear again, and again she made the translation. Her voice was light, confident. 'I am his niece,' Wendy said. 'Father dead, in war.' The two of them established a rhythm. He spoke, she listened, she translated, and sometimes Chang didn't even move to check our reaction. 'I want to work with animal. I go to factory. In Vietnam work-work. Eighteen hour every day economic miracle. Wendy chief sewing-machine. Mini yellow button on red trouser. No licensed doll, never ever. Eyes ruined making trouser for bootleg Mickey Mouse.'

Chang allowed his blind niece to stand and re-adjust her glasses, then turned her to face us, her glasses once more higher on the right than the left.

'I'm sorry,' I said, feeling the silence. 'I didn't know.'

'Don't be sorry,' Daphne said. 'It's not our fault.'

And then, because Chang was still looking grim, Daphne told him about her compulsive graffiti habit, and the condoms in London. She was a single-handed, unstitched pocket of resistance, believing every peddled illusion a wrong inflicted both personally and at large on the people. I blamed it on her age. She set such store in reality because she needed to be able to say, in permanent magic marker, I AM.

Chang's scarlet lips began to twitch, then he was smiling, his teeth stained red, and then he laughed, gleefully clapping his hands. He jumped up off the throne, pulled us both to our feet, then embraced us like a Frenchman.

'Darlings!' He held Daphne away from him by the shoulders, looking her up and down. 'Mmm. Divine.' He stretched out an arm towards his niece, like a master of ceremonies. 'Wendy!' She blushed and curtsied, then shuffled out taking tiny steps. She didn't take off her glasses. 'Sit down, sit down,' Chang said, fussing about us both. 'Make yourselves utterly at home.'

Now that he'd opened his mouth, giving away his theatrical landed-in-all-England voice, I remembered why I couldn't take him seriously. He sounded like an exile from an amateur-dramatic public school, and not like a radical French Chinaman.

'You two have arrived punctually at precisely the right place,' he exclaimed. 'Condoms! Fantastic!'

'Thank you,' Daphne said. She was flirting. She wanted him to like her. 'All my own idea.'

'And you, Daniel,' Chang said. He slapped his thigh. 'You sly old dog. I've been hearing rumours. Cartoons, isn't it? You're a sorry disappointment to Mummy.'

'Again.'

'And none of the rumours true! Condoms! I love it! New targets, more modern methods, just like I've been saying for years. Yonks and yonks. Aggressive irony, that's the future, very start-of-the-century. You've probably heard about my cabaret club? Same kind of idea. Very similar. And you know what? I sometimes do Disney, too!'

Chang was unstoppable, and there was never a good time to mention that all I'd wanted was a day-out of legitimate buyable fun, as globally advertised at enormous expense. And now, a place to stay for the night. Daphne was on the edge of her seat. She obviously didn't find anything funny about Chang's voice, suspending judgement by appearances, and I felt I was losing her. Partly it was the gun on the table, but it was also Chang's seasoned instinct for the one-way switch connecting hypothetical mischief to practical action.

'We have to take aim at the sacred fetishes of this age now,' he reminded us. 'Oh yes. Our contemporary monsters. Too many people look back. Stuck on banks and governments and the fat cats in the markets.'

Today's quite different and up-to-date and thoroughly modern enemy, according to an effervescent Chang, was the multinational entertainment industry.

'We could write pamphlets,' I suggested weakly, hoping to hold him back. Daphne had wanted to know someone, and be out in the world, but Chang was moving so quickly I worried she'd forget the way home. 'Let's design some posters. Hand them out in schools. Or something.'

'It calls for far more than reading and writing.'

'Poor old Daniel. He sometimes finds it hard to follow.'

'It needs a distinct, significant fact. Wouldn't you agree, Daphne?'

'I would. Definitely.'

'And you'd be right. Absolutely right. Corporate suppliers of entertainment are the twenty-first-century tyrants, re-arranging the world in their own interest. Now they're closing in on the internet, because they already have radio

110

and TV stations, cable systems, newspapers, books, home video, theatrical productions, computer games, even professional sports teams. They have recreation. They want to control the way we dream our world.'

'Entertainment,' I said. 'That's all it is.'

'It's industry. The end of the singular and the original. Individual imagination is gratuitous and unpredictable, yes, Daniel, even yours, and it's discouraged at birth because no-one can easily match it to marketing expenditure.'

'But it's not all Disney's fault, though, is it? That's all I'm trying to say.'

'Oh no,' Chang said, shaking his head with his finger held to the bow of his red red lips. 'Not just Disney. There are many others among the iniquitous. There are even other parks. If you think Disney's bad, you should see *Yurayama*.'

The recently-completed *Yurayama* themed amusement-park was closer to Paris than the *Parc Asterix*, but further away than *Disneyland*. It covered 2000 acres of old beetroot farms purchased in small lots by dummy companies, so as not to push up the prices. In return for 10,000 new jobs and four billion pounds of inward invest-ment, the park had secured preferential-rate bank-loans, a uniquely favourable VAT percentage, and exemption from standard employment legislation. The European Develop-ment Fund had also provided access roads and rail-links, both TGV and RER.

These expenses and exemptions were further justified by the extravagant promises of the graphic designer leading the project. His vision was of a panoramic version of the various historical epochs and geographical regions of the continent of Europe. Under its original name, *Europorama*, the park promised an experience which was ideologically coherent, celebrating and strengthening the core values of a Europe not so long united. Inside the park-gates, European history would resolve itself, the outmoded traditions of war and freethinking superseded by this new site of common European heritage.

The park was designed in the shape of a wheel. In the centre, at its hub, there was a replica castle. Although this was a recognisable device, already exploited by Disney, permission in this case had been secured in person from

Louis VI of Bavaria, to build a scale reproduction of his great-great-grandfather's real and original Black Forest home.

The elaborate castle at the park's hub was enclosed by four differently themed zones. To dissuade visitors from constructing their own versions of the European experience, there were suggested walkways and a surrounding embankment which cut off all views to the outside. When switching from one zone to another, visitors were generally channelled back to the castle, thus maximising contact with strategically located shops (over 50 in all) and restaurants (39, not counting foodcarts). This organisational model many people will already recognise from their shopping-malls and refurbished city-centres, spaces we use and move through every single day.

On the advice of focus groups, and with one eye on trade from Japan, the park's name was shortened to *Yurayama* (copyright-registered, registered-trademarked).

Each of the four zones was named after its distinctive theme. There was *The World of Culture*, *Our Ancestors*, *The European Dream*, and *Tomorrow is Today!*. These could be expanded at any time, or entirely new zones added, and every improvement would always conform to the founding philosophy of Better Living Through Political Unity. And also, Buying is Belonging. This was how history had resolved itself, in *Yurayama*, and the park's design was a tribute to the values of discipline and simplification. Most of the signs were in English, for example, for the sake of simplicity, and the finished park was a kind of architectural morality play, where the virtues of happiness, innocence, industriousness, and consumer participation comfortably triumphed over anger, indignation, bitterness, and critical thinking.

In essence, then, *Yurayama* was just a bit of harmless fun.

On a single summer's day, in its first year of operation, it had once welcomed more than 75,000 paying visitors. However, the standard daily holiday intake was about 40,000, and to cater for so many families at play the park functioned like a city in itself, though without drug-dealers or a library. Safety was a major priority, and *Yurayama* had its own security force operating more surveillance per square metre than many publicly funded prisons. As for the staff, they were employed under similar terms and conditions to the competing theme-parks also constructed within service distance of Paris. Most of them were students on short-term contracts. Some of them were Michael Millers, transformed by the pink-skied sunshine. And like everywhere, there was usually a wild Frank Babbitt.

Yurayama quickly gained a reputation to match its most obvious competitor, *Disneyland Paris*. In many respects it forged ahead. It was more contemporary, and didn't depend so heavily on rusty anchoring myths like Sleeping Beauty, and Cinderella. These weren't the stories which explained us, not anymore, and to pull in the visitors *Yurayama* had searched out modern myths with more relevance, common stories shared throughout Europe and freshly selected from filmed history and televised sport and memorable commercial-breaks. It had the celebrated indoor boat-ride *Olympic Gold*, for example, and the 360-degree surround-sound screen experience *Renault Fields of Fire*.

Unfortunately, in at least one area, *Yurayama* trailed in second-best. Despite the theme-rich resource of European culture and conflict, it was short of decent characters. *Napoleon Brandy* was always popular, as were *Beckenbauer* and *Mr Sheen*, but they were all too human to be lead characters in a park like *Yurayama* at the start of this recreational century. In all its publicity material, and on all its merchandising, and on the flags which fluttered from the elaborate turrets of the Bavarian castle, *Yurayama* was therefore represented, on a blue background inside a ring of golden stars, by two upstanding chickens.

Cocky Chicken was Europe's Everyman. His barrel chest and sturdy arms gave him a sense of completeness, and security. He was inventive but conventional, scatty but reliable, in a steady relationship but hopelessly bashful. He was an all-round nice guy, and Clucky was Cocky's girl. Clucky Chicken wore a short-skirted dress, high-heels, and eyelashes, and often had to cover her yellow beak to suppress an involuntary fit of the giggles. When posing with male admirers, she liked to bend one leg for the camera.

'*Cluck!*'

'*I* was going to say that!'

Yurayama had been creeping into all our houses for quite some time, on biscuit tins and babywalkers and tea-towels, on pyjamas and six-piece plastic breakfast sets. Public relations kept it alive and well in the pliable mix of mixed-media, praising the park for the money it made, though also for its added educational value. Criticism was rare, or rarely heard, usually limited to some unreadable PhD about the postmodernism of *Yurayama*'s creative methodology supplying an ideal template for the ideology of commodification. Anything both comprehensible and negative was probably against the law. Really. *Yurayama* was an acknowledged champion of the copyright laws.

'As it happens,' Chang said, 'I'm looking for a couple of volunteers to visit *Yurayama* almost immediately.'

'Maybe we won't stay after all,' I said. 'We should be heading home.'

'Immediately meaning when?' Daphne asked.

'Tomorrow. I was thinking Daniel's experience, Daphne'
enthusiasm. Both of you, to the manor born.'

'This sounds very suspicious,' I said.

'Trust me. I know what I'm doing. I've got a little something
which goes bang. I could hide it inside that doll of yours.'

'Oh no,' I said. 'No you don't. Absolutely not.'

It wasn't the best moment to meet Daphne's daring eye
the glistening black pupil, the liquid brown iris, the pal
shutter of the eyelid. Down. Up. This felt like my last chanc
to back out with any safety, to the comfort of the dull and
slow, sitting back passively, waiting to be amused. 'Hold on,
I said. 'Just hold on a minute. Not so long ago you wer
raving about new methods for new targets. Something which
goes bang is a bomb. A bomb is hardly very novel, is it?'

That spoilt, savage gaze flared briefly in Chang's eyes. 'I'n
fed up with being a joker.' *Yurayama* and everywhere like i
had no shame. Laugh at them and they didn't care. Chang
wanted to take the next step up, in the only language they'
understand. POW! KABOOM! #*!@#!

'Somebody might get hurt,' I said.

'Impossible. That's the beauty of the way I'm thinking
and what lifts my little bang up onto the podium with th
condoms. We'll put together the tiniest of tiny bombs. It'
not meant to blow anyone up, and I don't have enough of it
even if I wanted to. It's a warning, not an atrocity. It's a poin
being made. We're going to *pretend* to blow up the *Yur
ayama* castle, using a *real* bomb.'

Daphne was all daring eyes and excitement. 'It's brilliant,
she said. 'It's the latest thing. In the Florida *DisneyWorl*
they've opened this new attraction, which is a fake safar
using real animals.'

'Is that the same thing?'

'Please, Daniel, do try to keep up.'

116

Guns and explosives made me want to be clever. Daphne's eyes left me happy, and stupid. Down her eyelid, and up.

'It's the *idea* of violence,' Chang insisted. 'With the catch that we use *genuine* materials. It saves the gesture from overdoing the irony.'

'What's wrong with irony?'

'It's not very frightening,' Daphne said, 'and it's always so distant.'

'I don't know,' I said, backed into a familiar shell. 'I don't really understand. All I really wanted was a place to stay the night.'

'We're here now,' Daphne said. 'In Paris. We might as well do something.'

'Why?'

'I thought you wanted some fun?'

'How funny is a bomb in a children's amusement-park? How amusing *is* that?'

'You want something funnier, then?'

'I don't know.'

'Alright,' Chang said, 'cool your jets. This isn't the army. If you don't like the bomb we'll try something else.'

He took us downstairs, too early for more than a handful of unwatched acts in the narrow bar beneath his flat. Then it was down another staircase into an empty nightclub. I felt like I'd seen it before, even with the house lights glaring, and the chairs upturned on tables. We kicked up stale smoke like dust, while up on the echoing stage performers rehearsed in costume to a backing tape. The costumes stole the show.

'Very comfortable they are too,' Chang said, watching at ease in the military sense, hands behind his back, rocking on his heels. 'Hot, but comfy.' He suddenly jumped upwards and danced the steps of a sword-dance, hands above his head, then moved just as unexpectedly to the bar, where he leant on the counter and eyed up the optics. 'Not only can I personally vouch for their comfort, but I can smuggle one Cocky Chicken costume and one Clucky Hen costume into *Yurayama* as early as tomorrow morning. I have contacts.'

In the mirror backing the bottles he touched his nose, and winked. Daphne had to explain it to me. She was a natural.

As early as tomorrow morning, somewhere inside the *Yurayama* themed amusement-park, we'd collect Chang's smuggled-in costumes, find a quiet corner, and change. We'd magically transform into Cocky and Clucky, clucking and waving.

Then we'd break out into the unsuspecting park, and behave very very badly indeed.

'Why only two of us?'

'Have pity,' Chang said. 'My best days are well behind me.'

'What about Wendy?'

'Blind as a bat.'

That savage look of his made another flashing appearance, as if he hated himself for making a joke of it, then instantly turned the hatred outwards.

'I'm not convinced,' I said, but Daphne was looking straight through me. Easily entertained. Backer-out. Her rapt face said: spermless no-hoper from nowhere. Since London I'd sometimes lain awake at night worrying that for her fluent condoms she'd collected real sperm, without including me. She didn't think I was up to it. I looked over at the life-size Cocky and Clucky costumes, smiling happily and tap-dancing. I remembered the fun bowls of cereals, the perky table-mats, the biscuit tins, the underwear, none of which had been all that much fun.

'How badly behaved?' I asked.

'As badly as you like.'

'I could be Cocky,' Daphne said. She turned a circle doing the bouncy walk, with her bum stuck out and clucking. I laughed and stepped right to the edge. I'd been there on the cliff ever since she kissed me, way back in the bus station before London. I looked down, and Daphne was already dropping. From where I was standing, it looked like fun. I jumped, and once into the fall there was no stopping me.

'It's a classic idea,' I said. 'Fantastic. Brilliant. Except I should be Cocky.'

'Why should you be Cocky?'

'I'm a man.'

Daphne stood firm: 'I said it first.'

'If I can't be Cocky I'm not doing it.'

'Neither am I.'

'Right from the start I imagined being Cocky.'

'So now you'll have to change.'

'No.'

'Me neither.'

'Please,' Chang interrupted, 'please, people, please.' He held up his elegant peace-making hands, and minced smoothly between us. 'There doesn't have to be a problem here. You can *both* be Cocky.'

The next morning we made painfully slow progress, like children, wrapped in the murmurous lines of hundreds queuing. It was high summer, and the school holidays, and the weather above was wide blue sky and the certainty of sunshine. It was shorts and readable T-shirts, sandals, sunglasses, hats.

Disneyland Paris might well have been similar, but now we'd never know. This was *Yurayama*, bustling and alive and open to the public.

We waited a long time for tickets. Daphne had left her canvas bag at Chang's. She wore a white vest and a denim mini-skirt, her unlabelled trainers as always, and also the franchise sunglasses. I pretended not to know her.

Chang had given each of us a small key, and beyond the clicking turnstiles our numbered lockers in *Bahnhofplatz* contained Cocky Chicken costumes, just as he'd promised. Chang had a contact on the overnight cleaning shift (the aunt of the crispy-duck supplier who owed him a Citroen). Inside each locker, a complete costume had been folded into three standard *Yurayama* carrier-bags. The head, made of felt and plastic and synthetic feather, and rubber for the familiar yellow beak, came in two parts and was squashed almost flat.

We'd already settled on the time needed to reach our different zones, find the toilets, and change. After several impractical flights of fancy, we'd agreed to behave badly only in the zones we'd assigned ourselves. This was supposed

120

to overload *Yurayama*'s security systems, making our escape more feasible once we'd addled the park into dysfunctional, twitching pieces. That was basically the plan.

I had *The World of Culture*. For reasons of hygiene the toilet itself wasn't themed, so for entertainment I listened to urinal chat between boys, while pulling the stuffed green trousers and foam-rubber shoes over the tourist clothes I was already wearing. The barrel-chested upper-body was also in one piece, with the feathered gloves sewn onto the ends of the feathered arms sewn to the smart red waistcoat. All this had to be pulled over the head like a jumper, and Cocky was surprisingly stout. It was going to be hot work making a stand for the swindled classes.

I hadn't yet tried on the head. I sat down, I stood up. Calm, I told myself, nothing can go wrong because you have your lucky mascot. The talking Mickey we'd bought in London was sat astride the door-handle, grinning. I was still frightened. I'd tried to change but I couldn't, and instead of inventing cartoon characters I was now stuck in *Yurayama*, dressed up inside one. I was acting like my mother, who with Daphne and Chang joined the chorus saying there was no other way to complain. Most opposition fizzed out in the high-sugar solution of harmless fun, a chicken tap-dancing, a mermaid shrugging her shoulders. It became almost impossible to take a stand, to know how or when or in what tone of voice, because any objection surviving the fun was next-up against the trade-prejudiced libel and copyright laws, and the court-room foregone conclusion of *Dysfunctional Immoral Activists vs. Innocent Patriotic Chickens*.

I put on Cocky's head and it restricted my vision. It was like looking through sunglasses but also a camera, slightly detached, wondering what was happening beyond the edges. I suddenly felt quite at ease, one thing on the outside and another on the inside. I reached out for Mickey and hugged him against my padded cockerel chest. I took off the head. I made a startling discovery.

When wearing the head I was smiling and open-eyed and ready for anything, but especially a happy ending. As soon as it came off again, my cubicle was staked out by gendarmes crazed on under-cooked garlic. A boy washing his hands said, 'Thanks, Dad, this is the best day of my life'. I put the head back on, and felt several inches taller, like sometimes in my dreams. I took the head off. I was sweating. I put it back on, and two English cousins disguised as copyrighted chickens hardly seemed much of a crime. Judges, even French ones, could be allowed a sense of humour. I took the head off again and pictured Daphne in her sunglasses, feet up on the seat, patient like an astronaut, her own assembled Cocky head on the slope of her green-trousered thighs, all set for action.

Inside Cocky's feathered gloves, she wiggled her fingers, trying out the two crushed into one. She clicked her neck left and right, then pulled the smiling Cocky face over her own. She had clucked-out cheeks and a yellow-beaked smile. Her over-sized, white-egged, amazed-open eyes didn't once blink. She *was* Cocky Chicken, but then so was I.

No drugs, no alcohol, but Frank Babbitt sky-high on the rich red blood pumped by his very own grand glad heart of a scruffy old lion, you chin-chucking son of a gun, you one-in-a-million you. His irregular recruitment of Michael Miller, against all corporate guidelines, had been his first gesture of defiance, proving he was more than a character in a theme-park.

Now, to follow up that simple beginner's trick, Frank was back in the magician's hat. He felt fine and dandy, up and about. He was exercising his soul, bending and changing dodging manholes and collapsing cliff-edges, snook-cocking all those too many years of doggy obedience to his exacting employers. No, *you* swallow the dynamite. Yuck yuck. Yes, sir, giving Michael Miller that costume certainly had the approval of the duck.

Michael Miller was about to make his *Yurayama* debut as Cocky Chicken. He was already fully dressed, disguised to live the dream he'd allowed himself to dream. This is what he'd wanted more than anything, and despite suffering setbacks he'd struggled on, his tantrum in Frank's room eventually working its magic. That's what must have impressed him.

'Remember,' Frank said, 'whatever happens you're not allowed to speak.'

'Never?'

'Never.'

'Cocky speaks in the cartoons.'

'But you're not the cartoon Cocky,' Frank reminded him. 'You're the genuine real-life Cocky.'

The two men were backstage in a small room in one of the lower turrets of the Bavarian castle. From here Michael would descend into an underground tunnel, and re-surface not far away at Cocky and Clucky's temporary summerhouse. On a small stage the two lovebirds (engaged not married) would treat their attentive visitors to a royal waving welcome, while a security guard dressed as a farmer watched over them at all times. He could be found chewing a cornstalk, occasionally taking a camera to fit the whole family into the big picture with the chickens.

Frank sat on the edge of a table, his arms crossed. Their scheduled Cocky had been taken ill at the very last minute, leaving Frank to find an eleventh-hour replacement, and in the beam of Cocky's beaky grin Frank desperately wanted this to work. Back in his room he'd been cruel, making Michael suffer, meanly taking revenge for his own false promises made lightly in Paris. Now he'd redeem them both by defending the serious principle that Michael's happiness had the same value as any of the 40,000 paying guests they could reasonably expect in *Yurayama* on a summer school-holiday like today.

And he, Frank Babbitt, exercising his soul, taking something seriously, was personally responsible for increasing the sum of human happiness. He was proud of himself, him and his borrowed hat.

'Do the walk again.'

Michael did the Cocky bounce, back and forth, expert with years of imitation. There was no trace of his limp. His big sparkling eyes were level and straight, and his feathered hands identical.

'Hand over mouth,' Frank said. 'Good. Your face says happy surprise, and you're no stranger to happiness. Blow me a kiss. Thanks, Cocky. Now wave. All in the wrist. Excellent. Knuckles on hips, elbows forward, fingers back. Do the silent-chortle move. The rocking. Slight lean backwards. And the head. Perfect.'

'*Gee, Frank!*'

'But don't speak.'

'*Cluck.*'

'Enough!'

'That was my Cocky voice.'

'Not even with your Cocky voice, no. Do the walk again. Good. Now remember what I said about small children. Some will look frightened. Always back off. Also, they might pummel you and run into you as hard as they can. Remember they think you're a cartoon character, and can withstand anything. Remember you *can* withstand anything.'

124

'Can I?'

'You're a cartoon character.'

Frank checked Michael was sure of his underground route to the outside stage. Then he flicked some dust from Cocky's red waistcoat, reminding Michael that it wasn't just anyone who was chosen as Cocky. From now on Michael held the dreams of children in his hands, and the secret of the illusion that the character was real. Did he fully understand the responsibility?

'*You're the boss, Frankie!*'

'But don't speak.'

Frank patted him on the back and helped him on his way, watching him descend the stairs to the underground passageways, used by costumed staff to move unseen from zone to zone. Even down the stairs Michael was doing the walk. He *was* Cocky Chicken, and mostly to himself he said '*Cockledoodleoodly*'. Because Frank was wrong about the speaking. In the wonderful world of colour everyone gets to speak. Animals and birds converse freely. Shellfish convene debates. Electrical appliances chatter the day away.

'*Cluck!*' Michael said, quietly but firmly exercising his equal right to a voice. '*I was about to say that!*'

Cocky Chicken stepped out onto the balcony of *The House of Frankenstein*. From up there he could see the *Vasco da Gama Galleons*, and the ornate island rollercoaster *Rise and Fall of the Medicis*, and all of *The World of Culture* – *The Venetian Lagoon*, *The Magic Mountain*, *The Ibiza Bistro*. He placed a feathered glove over his smiling beak to communicate his amazement at all this that was his. In the medieval street, and on all three decks of the galleon, parents knelt and pointed him out to their children. Look, it's Cocky Chicken in his pressed green trousers and smart red waistcoat. Once everyone had seen who it was, they all wanted to know what Cocky was doing up there. Cocky had everyone's attention.

He smiled and nodded his head. He let the pause become dramatic. Then he rocked back and gave all his people the finger.

Elsewhere, Cocky Chicken has nice thoughts. Or Michael Miller has nice thoughts. Nobody knows the difference, not even Michael. Darling Clucky looks sweet as podded vanilla, and on the porch of our temporary summer-house we the agreeable couple make it a perfect day for countless grateful guests.

Cocky and Clucky wave, they sign autographs, they pose for pictures. Cocky with his two perfect legs (his elegant green trousers) he walks, with his two symmetrical hands (his expressive feathered gloves) he waves, and from the spirit-level steadiness of his bright constant eye he fires out sunshiny beams of the purest joy.

This isn't directly his territory, but Uncle Walt is surely watching. He's always watching, as wide as the clouds, and he gives Cocky a silvery wink and the thumbs-up, over-riding Clucky and the supervising farmer who both say it's time to go in now. Clucky playfully pulls on his hand.

'Cocky's tired,' the farmer says, moving the cornstalk from one side of his mouth to the other. 'Cocky needs a lie-down.'

But Cocky isn't tired, and his visitors aren't tired either. It's early. There are still thirty-nine-and-a-half thousand people he's yet to touch with joy.

Clucky cuddles up to him and puts her sweet Clucky beak close to his invisible ear, as if to whisper the corniest of poultry nothings. 'For fucking fuck's sake, Miller, fucking time's fucking up. Fuck off the fucking stage.'

126

Michael suddenly wasn't Cocky anymore. He was Michael Miller from Oldham, who couldn't afford to get it wrong. But he hadn't done anything wrong! He hadn't said a word! His every gesture made little children smile from here to the coming of the magic kingdom, and no mere farmer could lay a hand on Cocky. As for Clucky, she was a world-famous tease, already back to her familiar coquettish self, coy smile fixed in place, one leg bent, wholesome as a Greek sweet. Michael was safe, as long as he was Cocky, and Cocky could do what he wanted.

Cocky wants to walk about. He is so warmly received. He is loved. He can feel it coming towards him in waves, their love. They love me.

He bounces from the knee, blows kisses, shakes hands, signs autographs. He waves goodbye to Clucky. Bye-bye, my darling. He waves goodbye to the farmer. Bye-bye, Mr Farmer. He turns and poses for photographs (such a charming young chicken), but no matter what secrets the children whisper in his sleek invisible ears, he never once answers back.

Frank heard it first from his radio. Michael Miller had flipped. The excitement of achieving his lifetime ambition and dressing up as Cocky Chicken had supercharged his brain, though the details were still unclear. He was on some kind of wild rampage. He was in completely the wrong place. No, that was a mistake, because now Frank heard through the static that Michael was actually somewhere else, in quite the opposite direction.

'Fucking bastard,' Frank said, treating himself.

Minimising customer concern, he walked briskly when he'd have liked to run flat-out towards the latest sighting of Cocky, up behind the *Cossack Carousel*. Frank should have known: this was a plan approved by the duck, and the duck was famous for his inventive, eccentric, unassailable plans. They nearly always went horribly wrong.

Frank's radio was amending its latest announcement, which was already a correction of an earlier mistake. Miller was actually over by *European Space Mission*, in *Tomorrow is Today!*. Cursing, cursing, Frank changed direction.

Daphne couldn't stop laughing. This sometimes gave her Cocky an insane, buckled look. It was complete mayhem, and she jumped gleefully about, shamelessly stealing linzer-torte from small children, smoking a cigarette, stamping up and down on someone's plastic bag with it's classy souvenir Dresden China in. She skittered about squeaking '*Fuck! I was going to say that! Fuck! Fuck! Fuckledoodledoo!*'

All with a wide-eyed smile.

Security men in red anoraks would sometimes chase her, and they were hilarious. They'd suddenly stop running and press their radios tight up to one ear, closing the other with a finger. *What? Now?* They'd look at her doubtfully, then shrug, and all run off in another direction. Before too long they'd be jogging back again, out of breath, wary, working out for themselves that securing Cocky in an armlock was a career move unlikely to turn out well. Once, and Daphne just had to laugh, they dared lay hands on her. She screamed with all the indignation of an obvious innocent victimised and defiled (*Rape! Murder! Oh help me please, you good good people!*) until a handy packet of Japanese came to the rescue with their otherwise unnecessary umbrellas. The security men fled, protecting their heads, making urgent radioed complaints.

Daphne smiled, but then on the outside she was Cocky and always smiling. She cracked up. She felt invincible in Cocky's protective shell, the person she dreamt of being at last coinciding with what she was doing. She felt rounded and adult and ready to be watched, a wicked witch disguised as a cutey, sparing no one.

Daphne as Cocky had started from the women's toilets at the outside edge of *The European Dream*, at the banked perimeter of the park, beside the cruise-ride *Battle of Waterloo*. Either running away or just moving on she'd gradually drifted in towards the centre, like I had, whereas Michael Miller as the official Cocky had started not far from the castle, hardly moving since. He'd attracted an impatient crowd all wanting photos or autographs, or to stab him in the leg with a dagger from *Hannibal's Bazaar*. Cocky Chicken had time for everyone. He had all day and all night. He didn't need to eat or to sleep. A small child stamped on his foot. He responded with the silent chortle.

I'd begun my own sabotage by poking over a rubbish bin beside *The Heart of Darkness Steakhouse*. After my star appearance at *The House of Frankenstein*, my running-away had gradually taken me deeper into the park, in towards the decorative towers of the castle. However, I was now trapped by a park employee at the back of *William Tell's Shootin' Gallery*. His dogtooth jacket suggested he was somehow more senior, and he'd already pushed aside several of his younger colleagues.

'It's alright,' the man said soothingly, as if to a wayward child. He had an American accent. 'It's gone to your head but there's no need to worry. Come along quietly, Michael, and it'll turn out just fine.'

This was sensational, and very strange. If Cocky Chicken behaved badly in *Yurayama*, senior staff were trained to flatter him by calling him Michael. I made a run for it, the truth suddenly clear to me: I wasn't cut out for this. I was too stupid. I was too clever. I was a secret fan of cartoon characters and Hollywood's three-act idealism, and it didn't much concern me the damage these parks were doing to the collective unconscious. I was satisfied with the stand we'd already made, and now I'd like to go back home and watch *Pretty Woman* with the curtains closed, and without laughing once.

It felt like a good time to leave, which was when I saw Daphne in her Cocky Chicken costume over by *Palazzo Reale*, in front of the castle, surrounded by excitable children. I waded through, ushering boys and girls behind me like stems of wheat. I acted out fun as my emotional disguise, and threw my arms around her.

'Let's get out of here. Before it's too late.'

Michael Miller didn't reply. Frank had ordered him not to speak, and he had a responsibility to the children. Sustaining the illusion at all times, he hugged this other Cocky right back. Like Frank had said, he was a character, and there was nothing he couldn't withstand.

Just then Daphne, despite her different starting point, also arrived at *Palazzo Reale*. This was a raised mound of floral shrubs and concealed speakers at the centre of the circular rounding-off of *Gran Via 2000*, a pedestrian street leading directly back to *Place de Ville* and the entrance. All three of us, identically dressed as Cocky Chicken, broke into a round-shoed jog up the slope and onto the centre of the mound. We were running away from Frank, who'd arrived from the castle and was trying to hit us with a stick.

'*I didn't speak!*' Michael protested in his rehearsed, high-pitched Cocky voice. '*I didn't speak!*'

At the top of the mound Michael's happiness could just about withstand Frank and the stick and the two other Cockys. He gamely waved down at his people, and did the silent-chortle move, assuming there was a believable reason. There had to be, because inside amusement-parks all stories end well. Cocky Chicken by definition ends well.

Frank was orchestrating an emergency cordon of flustered staff, who were hastily joining hands to hold back the curious on the far side of the road encircling the *Palazzo*. For most of the visitors, already numbed by sensory overload, this was just another scene in the show. They either liked it, or they didn't like it. They stayed to watch, they stayed and didn't watch, or they turned away.

The three of us raised up at the centre of the mound were now effectively trapped. A small boy slipped beneath the human security cordon, in the gap between a walking tulip and a Viking. He was wearing an elasticated yellow beak, and at four years old he didn't much mind how many Cockys there were, as long as he could stare at all three of them for as long as he liked. And lick his ice-cream at the same time. Unknowingly, he was about to live his first distinct memory, made special by its imminent secondary association with physical pain.

One of the Cockys bounced down from the grassy mound, waving his feathered gloves from side to side, beaming his happy smile. The small boy held out his arms for a kiss, like the one he'd had earlier from *Schepi the German Shepherd*. Bending at the knees, Cocky Chicken came down to the boy's low level. He studied the child closely with his intense and vacant gaze. Deliberately, with his big, feathered, three-fingered hand, he cuffed the boy across the head.

Cocky punched the air and danced a mad kind of dance while the small boy stared horrified at his dropped ice-cream, and then started screaming. I didn't like that. It was within reason to spill some bins and make rude signs with Cocky's fingers, but Cocky Chicken attacking small children was a gesture too far. I didn't think: that must have been Daphne. I

131

thought: that Cocky Chicken's gone too far. I took a run down the slope and jumped, tackling him just below the shoulder. We both bounced to the ground, rolling one over the other, each struggling for a decent grip, attack and defence.

Michael Miller now knew for certain that something was wrong. Identical doubles were a recognisable cartoon device, but this kind of fighting was worse than wrong. It was evil. Cocky Chicken, no matter how many of him, should never slap children or fight amongst himself. He bounced down the slope and tried to prise us apart. Unsighted, we both pulled him in, and it was at this point that Michael conclusively recognised us as impostors. *He* was the real and only Cocky. He was also fully physically able, and there was nothing he couldn't do. He therefore fought back as if for his life, or for Clucky trapped by a cat.

Frank was the supervisor in charge. All the visitors and all the staff were expecting him to restore order. It was rapidly becoming another question of morale. He stepped forward and with the end of his stick (a bamboo from the jungle-fantasy *Lord of the Flies*) he gave one of the brawling Cockys a jab between the shoulder-blades. This was unwise, because one of the other Cockys jumped up and challenged him in a comical smiley boxing stance, offering the feathery defiance of his bunched and revolving fists. Frank warned him off by flicking the bamboo. It was only a warning, but immediately a howl rose up from the watching crowd. All sorts of people, all sizes and shapes and nationalities, were suddenly pushing Frank in the back, clawing at him, pulling him away from the chickens. They pleaded in several languages for everything to be explained to them, like in a film, but they also wanted Frank to stop swinging at Cocky Chicken with his stick.

Naturally, being pushed and pulled like this, Frank had to

defend himself, and so did other members of staff, and very soon everybody was pushing or pulling at whoever was nearest. It was complete chaos, even in self-defence. It was the universal outbreak of the duck which Frank had always predicted, and by the time visitors and staff came to their senses, only one Cocky Chicken remained. The other two had vanished.

Cocky Chicken stood deserted at the top of the grass mound in the centre of *Palazzo Reale*, cluck-clucking at retreating children. He was wagging his finger, shaking his head. He was telling them in his own special voice not to worry because all stories end well, they have to, they always absolutely have to end happily.

Children, do come back. Everything I tell you is true.

THREE

1. Top-quarter left – window: Eiffel Tower.
   Close-up: a foot in a wraparound plastercast.
   [dip pen, Perry Durabrite nib No. 16, Higgins Indian ink]

2. Hospital bed and chart with zaggy graph.
   A patient in comic traction, plastered all over, one leg
   raised on a medical trapeze. *Daniel*'s voice, off:
   – *Do you want the good news or the bad news?*

3. Window: the Arc de Triomphe.
   Close-up: *Daphne*'s fervorous eyes between layered ban-
   dage.
   – *The good news is that you have a week to live.*
   And also in the window, a shining sun. Beam. Beam.
   Beam.

4. Window: *Mona Lisa* (photographic repro, black and
   white).
   Three-fingered hand offering round-petalled flower.
   – *The bad news is I should have told you six days ago.*
   Fervorous eyes goggle. Trapeze snaps.

Also, I should have brought some flowers, but I didn't like the look of the flower-seller in the lobby. Empty-handed, in the clean and sterile space kept empty for waiting, I sat down and prepared for a wait. Facing me, the double-doors to Daphne's ward were security-locked, with wire-glassed square windows at eye-level. There was CCTV, and a security bell I'd already pushed twice.

It was the psychiatric wing. Several seats along from me a woman in a towelling dressing-gown ate breadcrumbs from a white paper bag, and occasionally glanced sideways. The backs of her hands were large brown blister-bubbles, over-doming the bones, the skin tight but also wrinkled, like the skin on milk. She also had a bandaged foot, and stitches in her neck. Coyly she looked across at me from beneath her eyelashes. She smiled. She'd stuck the crust from the bread like an orange mouthguard along her top row of teeth. It shouldn't have been allowed.

I looked at the bones in my hands, my hands on my knees, waiting on the double-doors to the secure ward in the psycho-wing of a private hospital near Paris. Daphne had been admitted several hours ago, arriving from the park by ambulance. As well as her physical injuries, which had stabilised, it was being taken for granted that she also suffered psychologically, considering what she'd tried to do. She couldn't have been all there.

With each fistful of breadcrumbs the fluid in the blisters

shifted, trembled, settled. A face appeared behind the wired glass of the doors, male, with narrow eyes under straight eyebrows and a receding hairline. It was a gym-face, squarely on the side of the many, the strong, adults.

He pushed out into the waiting-room, and I tried to remember that people weren't always the way they looked. He was wearing a dark suit. He smiled, all teeth, no bread. He was going to save me from the pain of the woman with her living blisters and breadcrust dentures and lightweight bag of crumbs.

'Hi!' he said, thrusting out his hand. 'I'm Herman!'

I stood up, and shook his muscular hand. That hurt. He asked me which one of the crazies I was here to see. I didn't understand the question, assuming Daphne had acted alone.

'There are three of them.'

'Are they under arrest?'

'Observation.'

It was supposed to be just me and Daphne. That's how it had started, and how we'd made a success of the graffiti, and the condoms in London, and even dressing up as Cocky, only the day before yesterday. But these others must have been true because a corporate employee called Herman was telling me their names, nationalities, ages, as if he wanted to make them real for me.

It wasn't Chang Chung-Jen and Wendy. A young white Englishman had lost a leg, below the knee, and also one of his hands. The other victim, an American, a little older, had a scorched throat and serious burns to the mouth. He might never speak intelligibly again. As for the girl, as well as some minor facial damage, she'd taken much of the blast near her fingers.

'Lopped off,' Herman said. 'Chopped off by the doctors. One from each hand.' He raised his eyebrows, shook his athletic head. 'All as mad as each other. Mad as hatters. No other way to explain it.'

'Are you with the hospital?'

'Not exactly.'

'Police?'

'No.'

'I want to see the girl. I'm family. Why aren't there any police?'

He blew out his cheeks, and clapped me on the back. 'This happened in the park, my friend. Own police, own rules. Coffee?'

A tired nurse in a mask and loose green surgical-suit banged out of the ward and said something nonsensical. The hospital was in French only, which had to be unfair. I stood up, wanting to get inside the ward, where Daphne was. Herman held up his hand.

'I wouldn't if I were you.'

'Why not?'

'Bedpan. According to the nurse. Want to watch?'

I didn't even want to think about it. The breadcrumbs woman smiled again, sympathetically moving the crust of mouthguard up and down with her tongue. I went for a coffee with Herman.

The hospital was designed like a wheel, with the lobby at its hub. Reception was in the lobby, along with a café and snackbar and shop, and self-closing doors to each of the hospital's colour-coded departments. It reminded me of a shopping mall, of Daphne's home-town, the amusement park, of everywhere and nowhere. Even in a hospital the pain was hidden, in favour of eating and drinking and shopping, and support-staff, laughing. That had to be a good thing, the better way, and I'd recommend they also ban sick people from the waiting-rooms upstairs.

In the rack outside the shop I looked from paper to paper, but found nothing on Daphne, or *Yurayama*, just like there was nothing two days ago after our riotous success disguised as Cocky. Was it really only two days ago? I asked Herman if they were going to prosecute.

'Probably not,' he said. 'We cleared up the damage. It was very small-scale. It might just as well never have happened.'

'You'll do something, though?'

'Why?'

'They tried to blow up your park.'

'It was a very small bomb. We'll be keeping an eye on developments.'

In French, Herman ordered us both a sandwich. I watched him eat, and listened as he explained that the incident was witnessed only by a tiny minority of *Yurayama's* projected annual attendance. There were no casualties, except for the three misfits, and prosecution would reward them with publicity, their only genuine aim. 'First rule of business,' Herman said. 'Identify the enemy. Then don't do what they want.'

'You said the other two worked at the park. How do you know they were involved?'

'It's a long story. You had to be there.'

'But you're sure that both of them were staff?'

'Not anymore. And I doubt they'll be getting a character reference.' Herman allowed himself a thin smile. 'Wait until you see them. Believe it or not there is some earthly justice.'

'What about photographs?' For some reason Herman was the kind of person I wanted to catch out. 'How can you keep it quiet? One of them might talk to the papers, or write a book.'

He laughed. 'We wouldn't allow it.'

Not that there'd be any pictures. This time I hadn't been

behind Daphne with my foolproof camera; I hadn't been there at all. She'd probably been relying on local initiative, and one of the many thousands of cameras in *Yurayama* always on automatic. She'd obviously forgotten the honeymoon couple in London, turning away from the dropped condom in the queue for *Planet Hollywood*. Easier to stay quiet, and unsighted.

'Someone's bound to say something,' I said.

'We prefer silence,' Herman told me. 'If it can be arranged. Silence suits us down to the ground, because we're the experts at noise, and colour. And at the moment ours are the noises and distractions on top.'

I stood up, and Herman's narrow eyes followed me, making delicate calculations I couldn't even guess at. 'Can I finish your sandwich?'

'Be my guest.'

Back at the ward, I kept my finger on the buzzer until a nurse relented and let me in. She was near the end of her shift, and I didn't look dangerous. The double-doors opened into a corridor, white green grey with folded sheets and surgical smocks on stainless-steel trolleys. The smell was plasters in grease-proof packets, and crystal-clear bottles of hundred per cent-proof, of getting better or worse depending on your last experience of visiting.

There were doors all the way down on both sides. There was also the unmistakable soundtrack of cartoon, whistles and bangs and domestic percussion. Every patient had a television.

At the end of the corridor, in the last single room on the left, Daphne was awake, blinking. I looked everywhere else, at the expected separation of floor and ceiling, and corners in the room at right angles, and a blank television on a wall-bracket near the door. There was an uncurtained window with outside security bars, and on a stalk by the bed, dripping, the slow-motion implosion of a transparent vacuum-packed bag. I swallowed, and with nothing else in the room left to look at that wasn't Daphne, I looked.

She was propped up between pillows, her head on a neck-brace like a plate. Her swollen lower lip was prickly with sticky black stitches, the surrounding skin stained blue with iodine or bruising. She sometimes had to suck back saliva from her swollen tongue. Her face was grey, hair swept flatly away from her forehead like a facewash. Both hands on the single sheet were thickly bandaged, like clubs.

I remembered from the hotel the varnish of her naked legs, like drumsticks, then not. Her naked arms, all of the naked in-between.

She tried to lift up the arm without the drip in it, her brown eyes moist with the hurting, but also, behind that, still staring and daring. I saved her the effort by making my unbandaged fist, my arm shaking slightly. 'Us against them,' I said. Daphne's mouth was too full of stitches.

She was telling me something with her eyes, flicking them downwards to the cabinet beside the bed. At first I thought she wanted to apologise. Then that she wanted me to pick up the remote-control. I picked it up, and aimed it at the television, but her eyes blinked rapidly and told me I was wrong. They flicked through the open door to the television in the room opposite, and the flickering blues of a permanent cartoon-time.

Her eyes dared me. I changed the other patient's channel. It was now a tennis match, but Daphne frowned mean-ingfully, nostrils flaring. I changed the channel again, to a financial-news programme, and then Daphne was happy and that was just typical. She was always going too far, as if even

144

now she believed there was something heroic in being the person to go furthest. Zapping someone else's channel once was funny, but she had to go that little bit further, just to make her point.

I turned the other television off altogether, and ignoring the urgent call-alarm from the room opposite, I closed our door. I switched off the light, hoping the nurses would forget I was there, surprised to find that outside it was already dark. I felt my way round to the far side of the bed, using my hands and the reflected light from the carpark beneath the window. I climbed up onto the bed beside her, Daphne my cousin, which according to certain books either was or wasn't allowed. I lay down, using my arm as a pillow, listening closely to her pained intakes of breath, wondering what she might be thinking. It was so difficult to know other people, to really get inside them.

I let my hand rest palm-down on the sheet covering the gown covering her stomach. It rose and it fell. I moved it and spread the fingers, so that each one filled a gap between her ribs. Still not comfortable. My hand glided to the underside of her breast, and maybe she'd have looked at me, except she couldn't move her head. Or said something, only she couldn't speak. Maybe her eyes on their own were tracking me, but I didn't want to find out in case just this once it wasn't a dare.

I moved my hand inside the sheet onto the gown, only one layer of over-washed cotton separating her skin and mine. She had a beautiful, fluttering heart, I could feel it, but her breast was disappointingly flat. I covered all of it with my hand, and for about the time it took to think it, I thought she'd been deceiving me from the beginning, just for a laugh. In fact she was a boy. Then I had another idea that this was a kind of test. Daphne was the secret to everything, and with

145

whatever I did next I could pass, or fail. I was on my best behaviour.

I kissed her below the ear, where the blood is always blue, but she failed to make an obvious and immediate recovery. So much for Sleeping Beauty.

146

T he happy ending had already taken place, two days earlier.

Michael Miller the undisputed Cocky Chicken had spoken out on the raised mound of *Palazzo Reale*. For ever after, whatever the consequences, staff-supervisor Frank Babbitt could rightly be proud of his exercise that day of an evidently autonomous soul. Daphne and I had successfully escaped, under cover of the mayhem, shedding our costumes as we crawled away between the feet of scufflers, then dusting each other off before leaving the park like innocents. We were both very hot, after the costumes, sweat and dust mixed, but in the train taking us back to Paris, blocking the aisle between occupied seats, Daphne had squeezed my hand, hard, all the excitement of the sabotage bunched in her skinny fingers. Their blood-heat stopped me from thinking, more effectively even than fun.

And that would have been the happiest ending, for everybody, and where it should have ended. Except that Daphne didn't count it as an ending.

We went back to Chang's narrow bar above the polemical cabaret club, and on the hour, every hour well into the evening, on the TV behind the bar, she couldn't believe the news had missed us. She wanted everybody to know, otherwise it wasn't even close to her imagined idea of ending well.

On the table between us we gradually trapped grinning

Mickey Mouse between emptied glasses. I asked her why she'd hit the child.

'There were three of us,' she said casually, lighting a *Monte Cristo* she'd cadged from a man at the bar. She was trying out smoking, deciding whether she liked it. 'Maybe it wasn't me.' She was also treating me like an idiot.

'I don't think the real Cocky would have done that.'

'The chicken freaked out,' she said, tapping critically at the ash. 'It was a chicken at the top of its profession. Highly strung, like a top racehorse.'

I smiled because it was easier, even when she told me she was the one who'd gone down to stop him. The performing green bubbles in my mint lemonade jumped and burst. No point making a song and dance about it. The past was vulnerable. There was *Yurayama*, and the *Battle of Waterloo* as a recreational scrap. There was the united destiny claimed for Europe, despite the evidence of centuries. And now there was also our flawless sabotage and scrambled escape – looking back, nothing could ever go wrong, except the disappointment of nobody having heard.

Daphne went to phone her mum, to tell her she didn't know when we'd be back. Yes, we were having a wonderful time.

From the next table but one, Frank Babbitt covertly watched her buttocks, first the left, then the right, and had to remind himself that on this occasion he wasn't in Paris for the respect of women. The bar was already loud and packed, but he was here for one reason only: to find out who'd borrowed the chicken costumes from the downstairs cabaret-club. Up at the park, even amid the chaos, he'd recognised the costumes from his frustrated night out with Jeanne, and he owed it to Michael to seek redress. The duck was animate and inflamed on Michael's behalf, and there was nothing he wouldn't consider by way of revenge. Literally.

Only this time it was as if the duck and the dependable mouse were acting together. Tracking down those responsible would need restraint as well as passion. With his fingertips Frank dabbed at the purple bruise ripening above his eye, thinking during his first pastis that before he confronted the cabaret he ought to make sure of the maths. He was right and they were wrong. It all added up. The *Yurayama* concept was pure and innocent, making its opponents mean and corrupt. This park like other parks was simple good fun, inoffensive and well intentioned, a haven for young people and the family. Anyone against it must therefore be embittered, over-sophisticated, and an enemy of all children and all families, everywhere and all of the time. *Yurayama* took pride in Europe's recent dreamy ideals, while those Jeremiahs who set themselves against it were jealous and cynical and crudely anti-European. Let's face it, they were an ignorant bunch of elitist public nuisances.

Also, and more importantly, they'd ruined Frank's belated attempt to exercise his under-strength soul. During his second pastis Frank realised he was frightened for Michael Miller. The shock of the impostor Cocky Chickens had made him even worse, the wronged cartoon hero already fantasising a revenge of steam-rollers, ACME man-traps, tempests. Frank felt responsible. He'd identify the real-life delinquents. They'd be arrested, pay their debt to society, and that would be the end of it.

Between the top and the bottom of pastis number three, the disruption of a single *Yurayama* day gradually seemed less like the end of the world. The bad behaviour of the impostor Cockys was a barely credible memory, as unbelievable as anything the brochures promised in advance. The press had nothing, because Frank had personally answered the few mainstream enquiries with italicised projections of advertising budgets. If it hadn't been for the effect on Michael, and also the young child (and also the mockery of his fragile soul), Frank might even have found it funny. Only fun was *The Battle of Waterloo* and *Crikey It's the Alps!*, with full provision for customer safety.

After drink number four Frank became helpless in his admiration for the girl attached to the earlier buttocks. Her bright Spanish eyes and all-round animation made him jealous. She was sat at a table with a man who looked stupid. And also far too old for her, almost Frank's age. After another drink, and a quick visit to the gents, Frank hoped she didn't mind him interrupting (this wasn't like him at all), but didn't he recognise her from somewhere? Annoyingly, hers was one of the few themes in the bar he couldn't immediately classify.

'Definitely not,' she said. 'Who are you?'

'I'm what happened in the States ten years ago.'

We laughed, but then we ignored him. I remember this quite clearly. It was the first time we actually met, face to face. Frank, the American theme-park employee, smiling broadly and forcing his luck. Too early, Frank, too early in the evening. It was a high-school error, most unlike him, but excusable considering the stress of his day, the fever of Paris, alcohol, the thrill of sex without good intention, the evasion of seriousness, and probably many many more from his backlist of easy fixes.

I could read him like a book.

That night in the bar in Paris there was a recklessness about Frank even more reckless than the duck, but apart from the duck and the mouse what else was there? The rabbit. Frank Babbitt the rabbit, beyond mortal control. It was snappy, demented, and came to him much more naturally than an investigation of the borrowed costumes from the cabaret downstairs. He dodged the audition for the gumshoe role, x dollars a day plus expenses, because through a mixture of intuition and eavesdropping he'd made a guess at Daphne's theme. She was playing at terrorists. Frank was an actor in a full-time entertainment, he could do terrorist. Motivation: the imperative for change. It was in his blood, and at that moment in that bar the American in Paris put his novel on the back-burner to ride his luck at cultural activism.

With the added bravado of the rabbit.

He pulled up a chair and leant across the table, informing Daphne that the global aim of entertainment multinationals, in his humble opinion, was to reduce all men and women to an average, blunting our adult faculties by denying us conflicting experience, offering us inane solutions that were a suckle and comfort, robbing us of future and past, leaving us like children, like babies, dwindled and decreased as human beings. *Honey, I Shrunk the Audience*.

Frank was on rocking good form. He paused to breathe. 'Did you hear about *Yurayama*? Earlier in the day?'

Yes, they'd heard about the multiple Cockys. Radical news travelled fast, to the right places, and Frank was in the right place. 'These theme-parks are the world in miniature,' he confided, making the revolutionary connection, accepting after five drinks, or maybe six or seven, that the sabotage of *Yurayama* had been *funny*, and that his time-sheet days were a lot less fun than today. 'I work there,' he said. 'I organised that sabotage. All those Cockys, I am their leader.'

151

It had the required effect. It was a theme which attracted our attention, a shortcut not to Frank the writer or installation artist, but to Frank the dangerously attractive incendiary revolutionary.

'How can you work there and also want to sabotage it?' Daphne asked. It was something about her eyes.

'I'm the brains,' Frank said, accepting the dare. 'I'm the man on the inside.'

Personally, I wasn't drinking, but Frank more than made up for it. Whenever retrospect made the Cocky trick seem easy, either Daphne's exaggeration or Frank's alcohol soon made it difficult again. Chang passed by. He laughed. He moved on. Frank then wanted us to blame the age's plastic presidents and prime ministers on *Bambi*. As long as they had the look, animals in Disney films could act unnaturally. What they did was therefore less important than what they looked like. *Bambi* had set the trend.

'Obviously,' Frank said, 'when you think about it.'

Then he blamed *Yurayama* for making the purpose and goal of every European story the inner-aisles of a shop. Disney was just as bad, and both of them had already been buying into sports teams. They'd soon be manipulating our games like they did our stories, as colourful lobbies to their shops, and when they had control of our games and stories then what exactly did that leave us? For fun, that is, for the avoidance of pain which made life worth living.

In between one outburst and the next, Frank ordered more drinks, or stayed thirsty by reminding himself in his sternest voice that to work he had to go in the morning. When he couldn't say even this in the right order, Daphne suggested we put him on a train. I glanced outside. The rain the French had wasn't much different to ours, and even though Paris had history and high culture, and Hemingways at every bar, it didn't have a decent wet-weather contingency drill.

'He can catch a train by himself.'

'Don't be mean,' Daphne said, standing up. 'Are you coming or aren't you?'

Frank Babbitt was drunk, wet, far from home, and about to get laid. It looked like back to his. The late-night RER squealed up close to the platform, brakes screeching some punctual freeform jazz. Exploiting some tested variations on you only live once, Frank persuaded Daphne to take his hand and step up from the platform. At the last minute, between the hissing doors, just when Frank thought good sense might prevail, the family-idiot jumped in behind her.

The train shunted forward, tripping Frank and Daphne into the same seat. Daphne untangled herself, giggling.

'At the first stop we'll get off and go back to Chang's,' I said.

'Don't be a spoilsport.'

I sat on the other side of the corridor, up against the window. Daphne now had hiccups, and she and Frank were trying to hold each other by the earlobes, according to Frank a never-fail remedy. Oh, very year 2000 revolutionary, I thought, very us against them. I rested my forehead against the cool glass, and did some close-up expressions with my reflection, which faded when we re-surfaced into a disjointed Paris losing its capital theme, collapsing into suburbs. The trackside crash-barriers were tagged with incalculable man-hours of graffiti, and out here the city looked more real, less photogenic, less fun.

Frank asked Daphne to promise him her hand in marriage. 'The will of the princess is her prince's command.'

154

'My liege,' Daphne said, letting go of his earlobes, crossing to sit beside him. She wasn't wearing enough clothes. She was fluttering her eyelashes. She was hurting me. I asked her for a pencil, and that made her stop whatever it was she was doing. 'Or a pen.'

She rummaged through her bag, taking out the Mickey Mouse doll before she found my blue and least favourite magic marker. She had everything she'd ever need in that bag, which we'd picked up at Chang's before leaving.

'Thanks,' I said, but then realised I didn't have any paper. I turned back to the stream of spray-paint blurred by the weather-scratched windows of the train. Was this fun? It had been, until Frank, but fun was only the opposite of boredom, not pain or jealousy. That's why it was always disappointing.

Instead of tagging the window, or shaping a cartoon at its bottom corner, I reminded myself we had nothing in common. Except grandparents, those who'd paid for that long-ago trip to Anaheim, California. Daphne wanted to grow up, and I wanted to stay young. I'd tried a pretend-kind of innocence, while she wanted life straight, as if by definition it must be better that way.

I drew a thick blue line round my wrist, like a seam, as if my hand was detachable. Daphne would have had it tattooed, and so would my mother. I went over it again, making it thicker. Among my stop/start cartoon memories Mum was the only person truly real to me, who could always hurt me. I realised how much I wanted to be real for Daphne.

Frank went to sleep. I had to carry him some of the way from the train to the exit of the terminal, and then we shared keeping him upright as far as a side-entrance to *Carnival Street*. I was pleased to see it manned, even at this time of the morning. 'I'll get us through,' Frank promised, waving us

155

away, and then taking several minutes to find his wallet. We could hear the beat of recorded music from the other side of the high wall.

'Nice to meet you,' he said to me, aiming for Daphne and frowning at the difficulty of putting his arm through hers, vowing as a man of his word that soon they'd be married, though probably not before breakfast. 'I know it looks bad,' he said. 'But that's not how it is. I love you.'

The night-watchman at the entrance insisted it was staff only. He wanted to see ID cards, because that's what he was paid for. 'Let her in,' Frank said. 'She doesn't need ID. She's Daphne duck.'

'Another time maybe,' Daphne said, detaching herself, raising her eyebrows at the sentry. He smiled, as if they each knew what the other was thinking: everyone else is stupid. Frank stumbled alone through the barrier, but by then I think he'd forgotten us. I was wrong. He re-appeared and waved.

'Nobody got hurt,' he said. 'Just a bit of fun. I love you.' He tumbled out of sight, falling back into the protected park.

Daphne looked at her watch. 'It's late,' she said. 'Let's sleep in the station.'

'Let's go back to Chang's.'

'Hardly worth the trouble. We'll be back again in the morning.'

I looked at her blankly. I was tired, blunt with recent jealousy, knowing she was outside my control, and always had been since the moment I'd first seen her, in her bedroom doorway in *Save the Tiger*. I could speculate, and I often did, but I never knew for sure what she was actually thinking.

'Tomorrow Frank's going to help us,' she explained. We turned away from *Carnival Street*, and the music and occasional cheering and jeering from beyond the wall grew fainter. 'You heard what he said. He's the man on the inside.'

'I think that was just bravado.'

'We'll make his dreams come true.'

'I bet you will.'

Daphne stopped walking, and held her canvas bag against her stomach. 'You don't think I actually liked him?'

'Be careful, Daphne. Not everyone else is stupid.'

'And you're not as clever as you think you are. Let's have a look at the station.'

'You do what you like,' I told her. 'I'm catching a train.'

I'd had enough. Dressing up as Cocky Chicken had changed nothing. In the recreational century to come it would still be them not us in charge of the recreation, we the ones simplified and used. We hadn't even made the news reports. So accept defeat, give up, be intelligent. Except for Daphne, failure was an incentive to go further, to try something new.

There were no more trains until tomorrow morning. While I found this out, Daphne tested the revolving stool behind the curtain of a photomat. The machine was in a recess, in a row with a drinks vendor and *Create Your Own Postcard*, out of sight of the nightwatch gendarmes and *Yurayama* security. She'd already checked for cameras.

'Pssst!' Mickey Mouse's head poked out from behind the curtain. 'We're in luck!'

Beyond the photo-machine there was a square of floor large enough for both of us to sit. She pulled me down beside her, and I crossed my arms, and my legs at the ankle, and looked up at the huge triangles of glass which patterned the roof, and some tiny white stars beyond. A deflated helium balloon in red and silver hung limply from a steel roof-support. Daphne pulled my arm round her shoulder, and

157

used it to cushion her head against the metal side of the photo-booth.

'We'll go in again as soon as it opens,' she said, making herself comfortable. I suddenly realised she was expecting me to spend the night in a train-station, like a sixteen-year-old. 'Isn't this great?'

Personally, I blamed the Walt Disney Company. If only it had been allowed, then instead of a corner in an echoing station, not waiting for a train, I might have been snug in *Disneyland Paris*. I could be writing whatever I wanted, as long as we'd loved it, and even now we could have been relaxing at the *Beaver Creek Tavern* in the *Sequoia Lodge*, enjoying a *White American* with *Chip 'n' Dale*.

'This time we're going to do it properly,' Daphne said, beginning to sound sleepy. 'With Frank on the inside to help us. He can tell us where they're vulnerable.'

'Not to bombs, I hope.' At least like this I could keep her safe.

'Definitely no bombs,' she said, closing her eyes, scratching her nose. 'Bombs are out. We'll think of something.'

'You don't feel like going home, then?'

If it wasn't so late, and we weren't squashed together in a forgotten recess behind a photomat, I might have explained that social change was over-rated, just one more shuffle of them and us, and all their familiar weaknesses. Instead, I told her stories about Chang, in whispers, and how he believed in cabaret only because he could never get bookings for television.

'It's his material. At one time he had a pro-gay, anti-war line-dance.'

'Cool,' Daphne said.

'The Pink Vietconga.'

Daphne snorted. And then, I think as a deliberate kindness

158

to make up for the many times I'd wanted to kiss her but hadn't, she turned her head and kissed me on the lips. Not for long, but not pecking, either. She moved back against my arm, tasting her own lips, closing her eyes.

'Fighting back never changed anything,' I whispered, the stardust nimbly glittering between us. 'You're not the first.'

'I am,' she said sleepily. 'And I'm ahead of my time.'

I pushed my head back against the wall, and stared up through the glass roof at the first silver ribbon of dawn. It was still there, the glitter, twinkling and glistening, shimmering at the corners of my mouth. I still needed to convince her that the two of us alone were unlikely ever to expose the systematic corporate exploitation of everything exploitable. But it could wait until tomorrow. The kiss was more important.

The next time I checked, she was asleep.

I tucked some stray chestnut hair behind her ear. She lived in a nice enough house which like the rest of the terrace had no front door onto the road. Come in the back door. It's not a problem. She had a roof over her head, and a power supply, and a cooker in the kitchen, and her own bed and a television. She must therefore want something else, really quite badly, something she'd repeatedly been promised, but which couldn't, after all, be bought.

Apart from the arm under Daphne's head, the rest of me stubbornly resisted sleep. By twisting my neck I could see across the polished concourse, beyond the escalators to some stacked pallets of canned red Cokes, and then the soothing progress of an early-shift African, leaning gently on his softly-spoken sweep-machine. Partially obscured, a billboard image of a man's white underpants: 'The Fundamental Rights of Man.' Through the glass up above, head pushed back, I saw beyond the limp balloon the dawn sky rippling into summer scoops of raspberry and grey.

159

It seemed an age ago that we'd taken the train back to Paris after impersonating Cocky. It was only yesterday. In the aisle of the carriage of the RER, after the squeeze of Daphne's blood-heat fingers, my hand had slipped out of hers and onto her back, to her lower back, and the damp band of her skirt. We should have ended it there and then, before the glittering curse of a kiss, happily ever after.

The bright wash of sunshine made me blink and cover my eyes. A gendarme was prodding me in the arm with his baton.

'*Reveillez-vous les enfants,*' he said. '*Vous pouvez y aller. Ça commence.*'

I looked up from beneath my hand.

'You can go in now,' he said. 'It's open.'

Daphne stretched out. Watching the policeman walk away, she made a yuck face, then sat up straight, looking round and licking her lips. She crossed her eyes to examine the end of her tongue, then pushed herself away from the wall. I followed her to a news kiosk, where she skimmed through the papers. There was nothing on yesterday's impostor Cockys. She said we were going in.

Before going anywhere, though, she had to take a shower.

After a brief discussion about money, we booked into *The Marbella Beach Club*, about half-way down the *Mediterranean Sea*, nearly ten minutes walk from the *Yurayama* main gates. Our one room in the park's cheapest hotel (in association with *Mastercard UEFA European Cup*) had a pattern of castanets on the curtains, and a carved relief of the curved European Cup as a feature in the headboards. It promised comfortable accommodation for a family of up to four persons in two double beds.

We were a family of two persons, and therefore would

need only the one bed. I let in the memory of the stardust kiss. Unfortunately, we had no plans to stay the night.

While Daphne showered I tried out the beds, and rated them one and two. Lying back on the best bed, I then zapped the channels for role models. Real-life television seemed slightly unreal, like the news, and after a while I settled on a cartoon channel and a standard three-acter, part animated, part live-action, the villains all-too-human and the heroes reliably cartoons.

Daphne came out of the bathroom. She was two-thirds wrapped in a yellow beach-towel with a border alternating famous shellfish and the crests of European football clubs. Holding the towel closed, she stepped her fingers through the make-up kit at the top of her canvas bag, open on the dresser of coastal Spanish pine.

'You'd better hurry,' she said.

I lay back with my hands behind my head. 'We're here now. We've paid for the room. We could take it easy, have a day off. We could stay the night.'

She disarmed me with an acted startle of her eyelids. 'For Cold, turn the tap to the left.'

When I came back out, in my pale-blue shorts, Daphne threw me a defiantly plain T-shirt, another find from the depths of her magical bag. She herself had changed into a soft blue office-shirt, with a fine herring-bone weave, which tailed roundly front and back over her smooth drumstick legs. The drumstick effect was complicated by her bony feet and jointed toes, the nails painted a chipped maroon. In front of the full-length mirror, on the inside-door of the empty wardrobe, she wriggled into her dungarees, then went looking for her unlabelled trainers.

'I've had an idea,' she said. 'In the shower. And it's not Chang's bomb.'

She was at the end of one of the beds, rolling up her trouser-legs, lacing her trainers. '*Fake* bombs,' she said. 'And lots of them.'

She flopped herself back onto the bed, staring up at the banded red and yellow ceiling. It would be like the condoms, she explained, only more so, and just as effective because everyone already knew what fake bombs looked like. Sticks of scarlet dynamite and a single plaited fuse. Bundles marked TNT wired to tick-tock alarm clocks. Fizzing black spheres, clearly identified in white capital letters, BOMB. After an anonymous bomb-scare, they'd cause total panic. 'Chang'll sort something out.'

'You can't rely on Chang.'

The beauty of it, as imagined that morning by Daphne in *The Marbella Beach Club*, was that nobody could get hurt. Except *Yurayama*, from the panic and the bad publicity. I towelled my hair, my eyebrows, inside my ears, imagining very many people not getting hurt, re-assembling themselves, turning back after turning black. From one calamity to the next we'd have squashing and stretching, slicing and dicing, exploding and smoking, but no one was ever actually injured. Everyone was allowed at least a second chance.

'First of all we have to find Frank,' she said, springing to her feet. 'He'll know the best places, and the best times to do it.'

'Daphne.'

'Now isn't the time to back down. Let's check out.' She handed me the Mickey Mouse doll from her canvas bag. 'For luck,' she said. 'Let's go and do something extraordinary.'

After a rapid stand-up *Sierra Breakfast* at the *El Cordobes Cafe*, we backtracked along the *Mediterranean*. Down by the shore some excited children dragged back their parents to point at the water. 'Look! Some creatures!'

163

They were ducks.

At the gates of the park we queued in the sunshine. Daphne put on her sunglasses. I bought the tickets. We pushed through the turnstiles. For the second day running we were in, and today like every other day *Yurayama* was business as usual. All evidence of yesterday's upset had been thoroughly disappeared.

This time, without the worry of a long stretch in an underfunded French jail, we could allow our eyes to follow the vista of *Gran Via 2000*, up and over the gables of the Austrian-style rooftops, as far as the soaring turrets of the Bavarian castle. We walked towards it, as if enchanted.

'It's a trick,' Daphne said.

'Thanks.'

'I'll show you how they work it.'

Each successive storey of every facade was designed on a smaller scale to the one below it, creating a false perspective, drawing everyone onward and into the park's far-fetched heart. For most people it was already too late: the outsized characters, the uncompromised colours, the rattle of accelerating track-rides. The hidden speakers playing childish tunes we'd forgotten we remembered. Very quickly there was no other world.

To prove our independence we turned left, into *Our Ancestors*.

In *The Forum of Ancient Rome*, I suggested to Daphne that we needed to talk. There was the kiss. There was Frank and the fake bombs. There was my sense of being steam-rollered, after meekly surrendering a perfect and paid-for two-bedded room. Daphne had a problem: she didn't understand me. 'I really was only pretending to be slow.'

We watched a chariot of the gods on *Mount Olympus*, clinging to the same tracked route every time it careered away, as many times a day as people queued to sit there, necks tight, happy to believe in a world which hurtled past while they sat passively strapped to a seat. It looked like fun. There was audible whooping.

'What's the difference?' Daphne said, funny lady, but before we could talk, before I could try to explain that being clever didn't mean I always knew what I was doing, we saw Frank. He was lower down across the water of *Fjord Vidkun Quisling*, and he must have seen us pointing him out from the masthead of *Ulysses Adventurer*. He veered away but we chased him, sometimes having to run, back through *Our Ancestors*, past *Ecce Romani* and *Hannibal's Bazaar*, past the smart bright queue-monitors at the luge-ride *Crikey It's the Alps!*, heading for *The European Dream*.

We lost him. He ducked into *The Mental World of Western Philosophy*, a maze made fiendish by mirrors and other avoidable obstacles.

Since then, more than once, I've wondered what Frank must have been thinking. He didn't know what to think. Frank, I can honestly sympathise. Perhaps you thought, just as a place to start, that we should have lived long enough to know that in last night's bar you'd only been pretending. It was a theme you'd adopted on a temporary basis, and nothing was expected to come of it, like all the novels you'd never publish, because you'd never write them. They didn't count, they never were.

Frank, I know you, I am you. To tell your story, and Michael's too, I've had to bisect myself. It's one of the oldest cartoon tricks, allowing the skiing bloodhound to pass both sides of the oncoming tree. Phew (looking back), that must have been close.

Bang.

*   *   *

Last night in Paris, Frank had been drunk enough to think he'd remember everything for ever, even when it was already forgotten. First thing this morning all that remained was his vague invention of an anarchist past. And the Spanish-looking girl with the buttocks who was madly in love with him. Oh, and finding it blissfully easy to get back home.

In the circumstances, he was proud to have made it in to work. He grimaced across wooden suspension-bridges, blanched by the mid-morning sunlight, and flinched from the sharp glint of waterfalls. Eventually, deep in *The World of Culture* beneath the rainforest canopy of *Lord of the Flies*, he found an empty dark cave, dripping with cool black water. His headache began to ease, and with it the hangover paranoia that earlier on he'd seen his new best friends from last night's bar. They were from his other life, in Paris, and things weren't supposed to get out of control like that.

Staring into a dark pool of cave-water, Frank blamed the park for letting them in. It hurt his head, but he could sense the duck rising up, spluttering and grumbling, and he couldn't drown him out. Drop him in the water and slam on a lid. He just crosses his arms and keeps on talking and sounds much the same, with bubbles. Ubbles. Lbbles. Frank blamed the park, where he had to earn his living. He blamed the park, which stopped him living themed and happy in Paris. He blamed the park. The resentment quickly took shape, quick-quacking, flapping about.

Before now, Frank's Paris method had always pacified the duck, and revived his ebbing soul. Only it didn't seem to work anymore. The duck was coming through loud and unclear, and to shut him up Frank needed more potent relief than drunken seductions in dated arrondissement bars.

He turned for rescue to the mouse.

All was well with the world. Frank would therefore leave *Lord of the Flies* with his head held high, resurrecting his breakthrough role as a regular amusement-park employee, reliable yet inventive like hundreds of others. With the sun honouring its summer contract, Frank found plenty to smile about, *Yurayama* and unlimited fun and the once-in-a-lifetime days of our lives. Look, over there, queuing for *King Arthur's Table*, a father explaining to his son the secret of success. Reach out for the magic of a product which everyone wants, and before you know it what starts on the ironing-board becomes a 27,400-acre self-governing mini-state, with more visitors per year than Spain. Yes sir, that's what it's all about.

Michael Miller. Now there was someone with his head screwed on. Don't fight it, go along with it. Swim in it. Frank beamed at the shops. So there weren't any bookshops, or ironmonger's for useful tools, or grocer's for ingredients for meals we could make by ourselves. But of what there was, even the smallest purchase acted like a miracle sonar machine, building up muscle without effort. If you're unhappy, buy something. Belong in the branded hat. Believe in the trademark Tinkerbell.

'That's where most of us go wrong,' Frank said, applauding both Cocky and Clucky as they graciously appeared on the summer-house stage in front of their many fanatics. 'We just don't go far enough.'

He meant these words for Michael Miller, who was standing right next to him. Insensible to the midsummer heat, Michael was dressed in the full harvest festival, the hat, the smock, the boots. The eyes, the limp, the plastic hand. He adjusted his floppy farm-hat, attuning himself to the irregular behaviour of other people, like litter-bugging, or book-reading, or home-made sandwiches. He helped a fatherless family pose their collective memory with Cocky and Clucky, then spied a gang of girls in the autograph-queue spitting peanuts over the ropes. Youngsters these days, some of them didn't believe in anything. Michael offered to help with a wheelchair, and pushed it directly in front of them.

Michael as the farmer had been Frank's idea, once Michael had accepted that he wasn't getting another go at Cocky. Not even after another tantrum. The impostors weren't his fault, Frank knew that, but he'd made it worse by over-running his schedule. At least as the farmer he could help to protect them, in case it ever happened again, and that was the argument which eventually convinced him. He calmed down, and yet again, it was Frank Babbitt to the rescue: he ought to have been promoted years ago, on merit. Then the duck need never have happened, nor Paris, nor Daphne. He could have been more like Michael. He could have been happy.

'You are happy, aren't you?' Frank was just checking.

'Tip-top,' Michael said, though he hadn't smiled once. 'Never better.' He wiped his hands on his costumed smock. Yesterday was gone, and for ever in the past. With a little effort, and a positive outlook even under pressure, it would soon be forgotten. Frank was incredibly jealous.

Michael narrowed his eyes and chewed on his cornstalk. The smiling could wait for later. He'd been crushed pancake-flat, but it was only a matter of time before he'd bounce right back. Characteristically, cartoons threw up many opportunities for heroic redemption. Vigilance was everything.

'You don't mind too much, then, not being Cocky?'

Yesterday, Michael had been Michael Miller in the body

of Cocky Chicken, and if it worked one way then why not the other? He'd discovered yesterday afternoon that all other Cockys were impostors. That's what yesterday's unfair incident had taught him. Today he might be disguised as a farmer, but he was still the real Cocky Chicken. Only this time he was disguised inside the body of Michael Miller.

Which was how he knew without any doubt that there was something wrong with the walk. He disapproved of Cocky's bounce. It had to be bouncy but not light-footed, carefree but not careless, and Cocky should never have been allowed out with a faulty walk. It made us all look bad.

He didn't mention it to Frank. He asked him what he wanted, because there was important surveillance to be done, and you couldn't leave the protection of Cocky and Clucky Chicken to chance, or even to staff-supervisors.

'I don't know,' Frank said, although there must have been something. 'You haven't seen a girl dressed in blue, have you? She's young, and kind of Spanish-looking. She carries a Mickey Mouse doll, and she's with a man, much older than her. He doesn't look very bright.'

'What have they done?'

'Nothing. Just if you see them, let me know.'

'Is Cocky in any danger?'

'Not that I know of. But keep your eyes open.'

'He is, isn't he?'

'Calm down, Michael. It's not life and death.'

'I'll fetch a shovel, just in case.'

Frank couldn't stop him, not without the risk of another of Michael's spectacular tantrums. He walked away, cursing quietly to himself as he skirted the castle. He cursed out loud. A twitch developed in his back as he cursed in funny voices, then different languages, words after words, rhythm without meaning, whackity-whackity-whack. Status quo? Status quack. The duck was back.

Opposite *Cambio Wechsel Change*, inside *The Craic and Ceilidh Bandstand*, there she was so very confident in her grown-up shirt and dungarees, leaning forward against the railings. She blew at a strand of hair, and smiled him a Cheshire cat. Frank escaped into *Swiss Cloisters*, the covered arcade, where a Belgian retirement couple were making eyes at the Clucky souvenir tea-service in the window of *Yurayama Collectibles*. They suppressed every higher function of the brain to make room for the message Love Me, Buy Me. It was such a sweet surrender, so consoling, and made these Belgians treasured the world over.

Frank, *behind* you!

We stalked him, hounded him, nagging away at his precarious mousey sense of order and *Yurayama*'s all-round-rightness, daring the duck to make himself known.

'Stop following me,' he hissed, surprising us by waiting beyond the corner of the *Amsterdammer Eethuis*. He stepped forward, forcing us back. 'It wasn't me. I wasn't that drunk. I'm not the father of your baby.'

He then apologised for the fleck of spit which had launched itself at Daphne's ear. She was English, he remembered, and that figured because the English were always the villains. It was their specific cultural contribution to the amusement of amusement-parks. Don't you know.

'Frank, we need your help.'

'You've got the wrong man. I know nothing.'

'You're the last of the great freethinkers, remember? You're one of us.'

'Am I?'

'You're the man on the inside.'

'Let's walk,' he said, lowering his voice. 'Anywhere. No, come this way. We'll pretend it's a Lost Property incident.'

He changed direction to round the castle, me and Daphne on either side of him, paying little attention to the *Breitling Orbital Balloon Challenge* or *The Scramble for Africa Breakfast Bar*, or even to the thousands and thousands of other people. Daphne confessed that in the bar last night we'd known from the very beginning that he'd had nothing to do with yesterday. Now, however, we could offer him the opportunity to live out some of those Sunday dreams.

'Is it something funny?' Frank asked, but only to satisfy the curiosity of the duck. He carried on walking. 'Like last time?'

'Did you find that funny?'

'In the end, yes. I read somewhere that fun is man's fundamental right.'

'It's going to be hilarious,' Daphne said. 'Much funnier than last time.'

She described the fake bombs, and Frank was tempted to give himself up. He could make a change, taking a gamble on the Frank from Paris, if that was truly where he was most himself. He'd take his long list of disappointments and rubber-stamp it with *Yurayama*'s world-famous logo, signed and sealed: it was all their fault. He fingered the welt in imperial purple well risen above his eye. Frank had to blame someone, or the mess of his life would look like nobody's fault but his own. He stopped in front of *Lost and Found*, next to *Lost Children*. 'I suppose you blame America.'

'No, not really,' I said, watching a fifty-year-old man in a *Brutus the Brute* sweatshirt biting into a *Thick Burger from Hamlyn*. 'In the end everyone's to blame. It's our fault for giving in too often to the temptation to be stupid.'

'But then if it wasn't tempting we wouldn't do it,' Daphne said. 'Would we?'

She was appealing to Frank's soul. She was asking whether Frank Babbitt considered his own autonomous soul more important than the giant international *Yurayama* corporation and amusement-park. Well did he or didn't he? He'd already come this far. He'd employed Michael Miller and set him loose as Cocky. Fascinated, like a matador, he'd held open the door to the china-shop. Now why on earth had he done that?

It had been his rare chance to make a difference, a stolen moment with the magician's hat. He only wished he knew if the hat could be trusted: wizards and dunces fell for the same style.

'You can be the man on the inside,' Daphne encouraged him. 'Come on. Be one of us.'

'I don't think so,' Frank said, his unique inner self all covered up, cowering inside the lining of the corporate jacket. Chalk up another victory for the mouse. 'I'm sorry. Last night didn't mean anything.'

'You were very convincing.'

'I wanted to be entertaining. I won't report you but I won't help, either. That's the best I can do.'

'Come on, Frank.'

'I'm sorry.'

This time we didn't follow him when he turned and walked away. At a guess, I'd say he went back to check on Michael, hoping for some reassurance that he'd done the right thing.

'It's not just the bounce,' Michael said, voice low, motioning Frank to come closer. He was leaning against his shovel. He took the cornstalk from his mouth and used it to point. 'Look at his silent-chortle move. There! It goes all pertly.'

'I'm not with you, Michael.'

172

'He's got it all wrong.'

'You are happy, though, aren't you, Michael?'

'I *am* happy,' Michael said.

Regrettably, there was always room to be happier still.

'So we'll do it without him,' Daphne said. 'He's not going to report us. He said so. Let's go back and talk to Chang about making some fake dynamite.'

'Just hang about,' I said. 'Hold on just a minute. I did your fun all day yesterday. Last night I slept on the floor in a public place. You owe me one whole day.'

'Do I?'

'The original idea was to see if we could have some fun. Remember?'

'We have had some fun.'

'Without breaking the law.'

'Half a day, maybe, if you ask nicely.'

'I'm asking nicely.'

It didn't begin well. The first ride we tried started in the dark, after a queue of longer than the fifty minutes displayed on a sign. Daphne pounced: two examples already of the truth being hidden from the swindled classes, but to me, and especially on *European Space Mission* at sixty mph upside-down in a hail of disintegrating space-station, the social question suddenly seemed less than relevant. Even Daphne momentarily forgot the wrongs she suffered, and those of the people at large, while I couldn't help wondering if for a modern girl like her this looping the loop was a sexy event. She treated it more like a test of what she could take, and she could take it.

On the way to the next ride she privately granted bad-conduct medals to selected *Yurayama* staff, rewarding barely concealed scowls and mumbled expletives, as proof that humanity would triumph. It was a short and inconclusive roll of honour, and despite everything I was yet to be convinced that the niceness of *Yurayama* necessarily made it the enemy. It was clean and safe. Nobody was poor or threatened or openly distressed, and if unreal meant nicer then maybe we could learn to live with it.

'At least pretend to have some fun,' I said. 'Blend in.'

I started to enjoy myself, thinking nothing at all on the *Cresta Fiesta* climax of *Crikey It's the Alps!*. Daphne must have been jealous, because instead of another go she grabbed my arm and pulled me into an archway between *Wonderful Wonderful Copenhagen* and the *Conquistadores Pizza Colony*. Inside the arch there was a wooden door, painted to look ancient, half-hidden by plastic foliage. She pushed on the iron ring-handle, and the door creaked open. She quickly nudged me inside and I stumbled down some steps. The noise.

These were the famous underground tunnels, and the noise was astonishing, and the sudden coolness, and the murk after the sunshine up above. All the generating noise of the amusement-park had been buried alive, the combustion of indifferent engines feeding kilometres of underground pipe and power-line. Here was the sum of everything excluded from *Yurayama*'s careful idea of an excellent day-out. Rubbish bins overflowed, wasted vegetables rotted. Lethal electric charges raced along the wired ceilings and walls. This was the miracle of engineering which made the illusion possible, but it was a black magic, without eyelashes. It couldn't sing and dance, and remained buried.

'This is the reality,' Daphne said, following me as I backed up the steps again. 'That's how it all comes about.'

But I wouldn't be provoked, and back in the fresh air I forgot all about it. It was easy. I closed the door and walked away, preferring the summer sunshine and the open-air charm of *Yurayama*'s flattened barriers between real and fake, near and far, now and then. Just as I'd always hoped, I at last discovered an under-developed tooth for the sugar culture.

'Daniel! Come back!' Daphne made a one-woman protest, stamping her foot, so I came back for her, dragging her along to the high-tech *Hot Pompeii Lava Ride*, where past and future subsided into the present. It was timeless, mindless, liberating. It was non-stop all-action fun, and nothing else mattered. It was even better than a bang on the head.

For anyone like me who was scared of life this was the place to be. There was no old age, and none of the dot-matrix greytone of hard survival. I was always the audience, and everything was laid on, and I was told where to look. I was told what to do, so I could never be wrong. My small world was made even smaller, *Yurayama* the first and last enclave of certainty on an increasingly unpredictable planet.

I was characteristically susceptible, wide-open to influence, and *Yurayama* had the benefit of years of practice at influence. I became willingly whatever they wanted me to be, amazed, pliant, generous. I lost all sense of time and place. I wanted to buy stuff, to show that I belonged, and to feel even better than I already did. There was no need to worry. I didn't even have to think, or if I did, I thought I was having fun. I gratefully accepted the offered illusion of freedom.

Waiting in the queue for *Icelandic Sagas*, looking forward to the shop at the exit and maybe a horned Viking's helmet, I was immune to Daphne's sly attempt at a counter-attack. In desperation, she tried to bypass my orphaned inner child by suggesting we acted like adults.

'In Paris. Here at the hotel. I don't care.'

'What are you saying? There's still *Ulysses Adventurer*.'

Also, I'd set my heart on a second tour of duty with *European Space Mission*. What with one thing, and then several others, it was at least late afternoon before we made it back to the space-port, were allocated an empty spaceship, strapped ourselves in for orbit.

To begin with, *European Space Mission* moved very slowly, the cars hauled up inches at a time to the launch-point, where they'd stop and settle. Dry-icing before lift-off, they anticipated the imminent 0 to 60 in three seconds flat.

Up crawled the spaceship, slowly does it.

Against the padded safety-restraint, fixed down from above, Daphne shrugged up, and then across. She must have undone a shirt-button, or even two, because the dungaree strap and then the collar of the shirt pulled away from the curve of her neck, exposing the band of her bra-strap. It was ivory, almost white in its flatness against her smooth and luminous skin.

I forgot about exploding space-stations. I flew straight past the swindled classes without even caring. Daphne the miniature grown-up was instantly my biggest influence.

'Let's stay the night,' she said.

'Where? Why?'

'Don't be dim.'

Daphne tossed the key-card onto the second-best bed. It hit Mickey between the eyes, and he fell over. We'd eaten the *Early Evening Special* at *Casa Luigi's* in the old town of Florence, before tracking back along the coast to *The Marbella Beach Club*. We'd been given a different room from last time which was exactly the same, down to the beach-mats for rugs on the floor, and the miniature bedside floodlights.

Daphne sat on the edge of the better bed, slowly unlacing her trainers. I followed her dwarf grey reflections on the TV screen, then lay down on the other bed next to Mickey.

'They nearly had you,' she said. 'You should be more careful.'

The meal hadn't been a great success. She wouldn't admit to luring me out of *Yurayama* under false pretences, and well before its 10 p.m. closing-time. She tried to laugh it off.

'Not funny,' I said, not laughing. I reached across our reserved family table, designed for four, and snuffed out the candle in the Chianti bottle.

'You deliberately misunderstood,' Daphne said, wiping her mouth with *Casa Luigi's* paper napkin.

'Not this time. I know it and you know it.'

'Know what?'

'What we know.'

A violinist interrupted with some romantic heavy-resin. Daphne suggested we concentrate exclusively on our next

178

defiant stand for the swindled. 'We should go back to Paris, tonight,' she said, but I could see that she was nervous, unsure of herself.

'We've booked into the hotel. It was your idea.'

Stubbornly, she didn't want to admit to a change of mind, but she was regretting that deliberate bra-strap. At last I had evidence of wavering, a point of weakness. I decided to take advantage, otherwise what was cleverness for?

'What about that thing you did with your shoulder?'

'What thing?'

'On *European Space Mission*.'

'An itch,' Daphne said, forking through her fascinating spaghetti. 'It could happen to anyone.'

'And the hotel?'

'I was tired. Last night I slept in a train station.'

Back in the hotel-room, she was taking forever to unlace her trainers, but in amusement-parks generally the passing of time is selective. It's a hundred years ago, it's life in the solar system, with no great warp in between. It's Daphne stalling for time, leaning forward, fiddling with her shoes. I looked down the front of her shirt. Under the influence of the park I was a child again, amazed by the suspended animation of flesh outpressing the lace of her bra, faded to the colour of teeth.

She jerked upright and kicked off her shoes, and I picked important fluff off the Castilian bedspread.

'Jesus, Daniel.'

'What?'

'You were looking down my shirt.'

'Was I?'

'Grow up.'

She stood and walked barefoot into the bathroom, and I stared after her in a kind of daze. For me it was spring again, and the dew was out all over, and the century was fresh.

Daniel and Daphne, that was the point of every new century. I had park fever. It was at work on my fantasies, approving my childish crush on Daphne.

From the bathroom, running water.

This was dangerous and stupid territory, again. Under the spell of the park I could be young, and not grown-up, and always about to inherit the earth. I could have the fun of living out my dreams, and unlearning the phrases lying in wait for twenty-eight and ever after: 'Better not', 'You never know', 'Where's it going to end?'.

Touched by *Yurayama*, I preferred Daphne's 'we only live once', 'we can do anything'. She wanted to grow up, to risk dealing with whatever turned out to be real, and if only she'd lie down next to me, we could both have exactly what we wanted. There was nothing to fear. In years to come, in the spirit of the age, we'd look back and laugh. 'Oh God!' she'd scream, uncorking bottle number two with a flourish. 'And remember? I pretended I didn't even want to!'

Daphne re-appeared in the doorway of the bathroom, the water now stopped, still fully dressed apart from her shoes. She had her hands in her pockets. 'What's got into you?'

'It was fun, wasn't it? Admit it.'

Yurayama had to work, or else. Or else it was rubber masks and tying people up. It was ever more extreme acts to counter the boredom, hoping fun was the same as pleasure, or at best an approximate opposite to pain.

'Their type of fun's for kids,' Daphne said. 'And by the way, I'm not frightened.'

'Of what?'

She unbuttoned the two shoulder-straps of her dungarees, and let the top half drop. She tugged out the tails of her man's blue shirt, crossed her hands beneath her waist, and pulled it up and over her head.

180

Stop that panel. Go back. *Go back.*

Stop. In perspective, the straighter of her legs was slightly further away, and therefore receding. The bending leg was closer, and therefore advancing. Her belly button and her stomach and her drumskinned ribs each had their light and their dark as the shirt insided-out and covered her face, her hands crossed at the curved hem as her neck arched through. Every part of her was either advancing or receding, converging always on a single point, where perspective famously vanished.

As I'd already discovered, on three separate occasions, she favoured underwear in glossy fabrics, the colour of teeth. She dropped the shirt to the floor, then pushed down her trousers, stepping out of the dungarees and walking to the dresser, in stripped Atlantic pine. She leant back against it, taking her weight on her hands, fingers straight and pointing backwards, something bold and almost foolhardy in the baring of the soft inside of her arms. She wasn't at all relaxed, her shoulders a forced line parallel with the floor and the stormy blood-and-yolk ceiling, the skin dipped above her tensed collar-bones, which threatened the flatness of the vertical ivory bra-straps.

'It has to be a real bomb,' she said.

'Daphne, don't. Not now.'

She chewed on her lower lip, placing one of her feet on top of the other. 'You see my point, though, don't you? It's time to stop messing around. Having a laugh. The only way through all this flim-flam is with something unshakeably real.'

I wondered how much of this bluster was brought on by standing half-naked in only her underwear. 'Count me out. I said so at Chang's.'

'Otherwise it's fakes of fakes until there's nothing left.' She tapped her two front teeth with her nails. 'We can use Chang's bomb. It's tiny. No one gets hurt.'

'It's a definite no. The park's crawling with small children.'

She rubbed the inside of one knee against the inside of the other, the heel of one foot lifting. 'So boom. Except for a tiny pair of pink or blue shoes, smouldering.'

'Not funny.'

She crossed her arms, beneath, above, uncrossed them, flat-palmed her own stomach, re-crossed her arms. 'A real bomb,' she said. 'To counteract all these synthetics, like a timely reminder.'

It was a kind of madness, like a closing-down sale: everything must go. Daphne genuinely ached for disillusion, as fervently for an end to *Yurayama* and *The Marbella Beach Club* as to everything else that was so patently unrecognisable. There'd be no gun at Chang's, or at best only a replica, and even an end to faking her age with make-up, and me faking it as a stupid cartoonist. She'd make me confess that in a novel it wasn't fair play to refuse to talk about my mother, just because I didn't want to. I'd have to look back, and despite my short-contract life simplified into cartoon strips, admit that Mum stayed real because she caused me pain.

I'd failed her, and then I'd blamed her for it, which hurt me. She hurt me by being right, so that to live an original story of my own I had to be wrong. I pretended to be slow, and embraced cartoons, where her earnestness had no power. Daphne had then reminded me of love, that rare incidence of realism without pain. And now I had no idea if she loved me back, but I did know the only sure way of being real for her.

'Don't make me explain,' she said. 'It's just what I feel.'

'We've done more than enough,' I said. 'Come and lie on the bed.'

'I'm happy where I am.' She shifted her hips, examined the ceiling, then the top of her shoulder, pushing out her lower lip. She spotted something she didn't like, and brushed it away.

'Frightened?'

'Condoms.'

'I never said that. I never even suggested it.'

'It's like the bomb. It's your version of something real.'

'I haven't once mentioned it, have I?'

'Alright then,' she said, fixing me with her almond eyes, half-closed. 'But don't you dare touch me.'

She came across to the end of the bed, and climbed on. First her hands, then her knees. She rolled over and curled herself up, turned away from me, hands clamped inside her armpits.

I lay behind her, consulting the shiny clips of her backbone, counting upwards, then back again. She loves me, she loves me not, sex, violence, the inaccurate alternating current of realist fictions.

'You're right,' I said. 'Not everything can be funny all the time.'

I reached out my index finger to touch her spine, but before I made contact she turned over. On this side of her, instead of a vertebra, if I hadn't pulled back my finger, I'd have touched a small dot slightly above the central bow of her glossy bra, a sunspot, where God's felt-tip must have slipped. I could have rubbed it off, but in retreat my hands had flatly joined in prayer between my knees. Daphne was very close. She smelled honest, like toast. She'd never be the one to fake it, or *I Love You*.

She said, almost a regret: 'Not everything can stay pretend.'

She leant towards me, over me, and plucked the Mickey

183

Mouse from the bed behind my back. She clutched him against her chest, her throat, and stared at nothing, somewhere downcast between us. Her lower lip began to tremble, like water. Then it went, and that was it. She was crying, like a child, like a baby. The amusement-park had found her out.

'Daphne, please. Don't cry.'

I wanted to touch her, like an adult. See it my way, and stop being a baby, which I know is what you want. Touch me like a grown-up. Please. And then she nearly had my lip going, too, and I had to half-swallow a gulped pebble of self-pity. I rescued myself with rapid emergency thinking, plastic and buoyant. Tears couldn't be allowed to make any difference. Life without illusions was the undecorated animal intelligence of eating, sleeping, fighting, fucking. Everything was allowed, absolutely everything. Most of it was probably fun. That's what she always said she wanted.

'I'm sorry,' Daphne sniffed.

'No, I'm sorry.'

She swallowed hard and stiffened her lips, wiping her eyes on Mickey's absorbent ears. 'Turn off the light.'

I turned it off and came back to the bed, suddenly made afraid by the dark. How could I trust her if I couldn't see her? She might be laughing at me, after reading my mind. After some expert tearful play-acting. I lay down in the opposite direction to before, my eyes adjusting to the shape in the headboard of the high-handled European trophy. She pushed up against me, her front squeezed against my back, dazzling me with the flashlit fantasy of actually being her, becoming Daphne, reckless and fantastic. She banged her forehead slowly and rhythmically against the back of my neck. God knows what she was thinking, which was all I ever needed to make her human, to know what she and other people were really thinking.

184

It was a long time since we'd left the park. The effects were wearing off, and with it the fever, and the freedom of my Daphne fantasy. It was suddenly worse than childish, and more complicated than a simple cutback to the happy ending. I couldn't begin to cope with the hurt, the pain, with making things real.

She touched me, as I'd imagined it, thinking the more tolerant books might allow this of cousins, as long as it didn't become a habit, and probably remained a secret. Too much thinking, not enough fun, even though in the too short time it lasted I knew it was fake. I was always outside of her, and turned away from her. It was a substitute, like the idea of the fake bombs, without the courage to make it real.

I lay awake in the dark for a long time afterwards, already missing her hands, trying to picture it.

An hourglass, flat at top and bottom.

Behind me, she slept.

As one shoulder dips, the hip on the same side rises. Repeat.

The next morning I woke in a dream with Chang Chung-Jen in the dragon-lacquered box of his Chinese room. An organic black mouse scratched between our shoes. A plump mallard waddled this way and that. Chang picked it up and stroked the green of its head. He aimed the gun directly between its eyes.

'I shoot several of God's creatures every day. Whichever proves the least entertaining.'

Daphne, eyes flashing, announced her undying admiration for the Vietnamese, their country chosen by history, risking all for glory against the imperial American pigs.

'I'm basically Chinese,' Chang said. 'We pretend we weren't there.'

I went back to sleep and woke up in another dream, me with Daphne, neither of us wearing any clothes. I woke out of that dream and now I was awake, and Daphne was dressed and gone.

I found her in the hotel's vast self-service restaurant, *The Stadium of Light*, eating a *Continental Breakfast*.

'I'm going back to Paris,' she said. 'To see Chang. You probably don't want to come.'

'Daphne.'

She refused to look at me, making the butter and bread of her breakfast a compelling business. Not wanting to leave the table to fetch my own, I drank some of her juice. That made her look.

'Last night,' I said.

'I got carried away.'

'No, it was me. It was the park. It made me childish.'

'I mean the bomb.' As if she could never have meant anything else. 'Fake is just fine.'

'Let me help.'

'No point. You've already had your reward.'

'That's not fair.'

She was reaching the end of her breakfast, the heel of a roll, a mouthful of coffee. I considered violence. I was a man and she was a woman, big against small, the world without illusions. I could have dragged her from *The Stadium of Light* by the ligaments in her wrist, cheered on by the zealous faces of the painted spectators. Last night, talking about the bomb, we'd already established that violence was a type of ending, but the morning after I wasn't cartoonish enough to find out what type exactly would follow on from giving Daphne a slap. I considered *I Love You*, but my own version seemed laughably complicated, especially in a place as simplified as this.

'I'm going now,' she said. 'I want to get it done today.'

'I love you.'

'You're a grown man, Daniel. Don't act as stupid as you look.'

'At least let me come with you in the train.'

I paid the hotel and breakfast bill, and for the RER tickets back to Paris, and this time on the train I stared between my feet at the grease of gum-stains. I was wondering what had happened to the spell of the park, because travelling away from it I felt old, and guilty, and constrained. On the Paris platform, wondering how to say goodbye, none of the magic had lingered. There was no stardust to keep Daphne back from the barriers down to the Metro.

She was going, gone through the barrier and on towards the escalator. She was standing still, descending, not looking back, leaving nothing behind. She even took our Mickey Mouse, stuffed head-first into her canvas bag, as if she'd be the one in need of luck.

For some time I just stood there, imagining other endings.

Then I went looking for timetables. Above the RER ticket office I studied a screen of arrivals and departures, making a decision without too much thinking, impulsive, spontaneous, and a small insurgence in itself against the proscribed paths of all our *Yurayama* futures.

I changed platforms. I boarded the next Line A train leaving Paris to the east, via the stations of *Auber* and *Châtelet Les Halles* and *Gare de Lyon*, stopping and starting in the direction of *Chessy Marne-la-Vallée*. Without Daphne I was bereft, in another world, and my destination was *Disneyland Paris*.

This is Europe, land of the free.

It took about half an hour, and they'd ordered nobody to the terminus to stop me. I rode the steel escalator, left the station, followed the engraved rose-granite hexagons of *Promenade Disney*. For the first time in ages an ache slowly returned in the shape of the hole in my tooth. At the ticket kiosks and the turnstiles I kept quiet and paid my money. I was in, blinking like a long-distance traveller, scarcely able to believe I'd made it.

This is not the story. These are just accurate facts I'm reporting of my day in *Disneyland Paris*, after Daphne left me. That's allowed.

Whatever she'd said at breakfast, I think I understood even then that Daphne never intended to ask Chang Chung-Jen for very many fake bombs. And unless he'd already had them in stock, perhaps for one of his shows, he couldn't possibly have made them up in a single day. It wasn't, therefore, a realistic idea. So at about the same time as I was in *Disneyland Paris*, admiring the summer sunshine saturating the coloured-in colours of *Main Street USA*, Daphne would have been upstairs in Chang's flat, keeping him to his word, asking him to pack Mickey Mouse with the boasted explosive.

'Right now, if you can. I want to do it today.'

Chang could, and he did. It was a small bomb, easily done, not even troubling his lizard-green nail-varnish, which he was wearing today to match the silk of his tunic. He made a flutter of his hands while warning Daphne that the string in Mickey's back would only pull out once. 'After that, as soon as it starts rewinding, you can stop it where it is but you can't pull it out again. You can't cut it either, because the mechanism inside the body winds back anyway, even without the string, so the detonator would still engage.'

'What happens if I pull out the cord and then change my mind?'

'Don't change your mind, my darling.'

As for me, I set out to spend the day, far from happy with the ending of my story with Daphne. I used up a morning of my life at *Disneyland Paris* in the midsummer sunshine, recognisable and real and rooted to the truth of our own known world. I was back where I'd started, and in the elaborate store-windows of *Main Street USA* I saw money. That was real enough, money and the glumness of the dazed, glassy-eyed faces passing me by. *Disneyland Paris* was a first resort for families in trouble, and often it showed. I saw only one other single man, a little older than me, looking bemused, and therefore English. A surveyor, I guessed, who'd worked as a trainee on project *EuroDisney*, when under construction it had looked like the

189

moon. He was remembering an excited sign: *Opening!*
Spring 1992! Meet All Your Childhood Heroes! And
now he was back, looking everywhere for the swash of
Sir Vivian Richards.

God my capacity for stupidity. I had no right to be
imagining other people's Disneyland experience. How
should I know why they were here?

I resisted the perspective trick of *Main Street*, tempting
me on with everyone else towards *Sleeping Beauty's Castle*.
As a minor act of defiance, in honour of Daphne, I turned
left.

And found myself in *Frontierland*. Mock paddle-steamers
on a man-made *Mississippi* circled *Thunder Mountain* on
hidden underwater tracks. Further on, the purple shell of
Phantom Manor rattled and cackled with mechanical ghosts.
I saw a jail, a saloon, cavalry quarters, and the teepees of an
Indian village. These were no less fake than the ghosts,
despite once being real.

Resistance was useless. Following the paths laid down, I
soon found myself back at the castle, only this time arriving
from the side. I sat down on a stone bench in front of *Castle*
Stage, and joined the audience for Mickey and Minnie.
Mickey was in his black tailcoat and red trousers, his round
foam-rubber shoes. He had the familiar widow's peak and
the broad pink nose, creased up in the middle. Everyone
knows the painted eyebrows, the rosy cheeks, the black glass
eyes. The perfectly circular ears.

He blew kisses, waved, chuck-chuckled into his white and
immaculate gloves, always smiling like a benign but simple
uncle, constantly on the verge of an expansive but mean-
ingless wink.

I wondered about Daphne. I imagined her outside the
gates of *Yurayama*, waiting for the decoy of the parade.

Fanfare, of course, trumpets. Time for the *Yurayama* parade of the day.

Standing up from his throne on the leading float, coming our way, the star character with his even-eyed gaze, his gloved expressions of wave and kiss. Cocky Chicken danced a sprightly jig on his cheerful little legs, two hundred per cent himself again, and visibly up for the show. Music, maestro, please: *If I Was A Cockerel, As Time Crows By, These Fowlish Things*. Let the grand finale begin.

Inside the main gates, Frank Babbitt was supervising security checks on stragglers pushing hard through the brushed steel of the turnstiles. Dads back from *The Marbella Beach Club* just in time with a forgotten camera. It's the parade, dummy, you always ruin everything!

The turnstiles offered only token resistance, then rolled over. 'Oh shucks, alright,' they clickety-clicked, because that was their job, to let people in. 'Oh shucks, oh shucks,' they said, and then there she was, in again, bag on her shoulder and doll in her hands, faded in blue from her trainers through her skirt to *Save the Tiger*, her eyes drawn along the funnel of *Gran Via 2000*, up to the swelling turrets of the Bavarian castle. I could see it all, and everything would turn out fine. Of course it would. Like Michael, I couldn't imagine it ending otherwise, not in a children's amusement-park.

On the park-side of the turnstiles a security man in his red anorak closed in on Daphne. A great surge of relief, like an opening curtain, swept aside the tension in my chest. As predicted, this story too was about to end happily. They'd search her and suspect the heaviness of the doll, and she'd have to hand it over, break down in tears, confess everything.

Frank called out to his colleague, diverting his attention,

191

then he winked at Daphne and waved her through. It all happened as quickly as the beating of his heart, this proof that he was truly alive. He was helping to sabotage a children's amusement-park. Take that, duck! This marked the end of his childish ways, and Daphne's fake bombs were all set to be seriously funny.

My chest cramped up again. Daphne smiled her thanks to Frank, then lost herself in the sway and hum of other people, different people from yesterday but also still the same.

The parade was moving ever closer, the music grooved in its repeating pattern of again and again. Cocky and Clucky's leading float, trailing the tail of the parade behind it, had started its journey out at the perimeter, beside the cruise-ride *Plus Ça Change*. It had lumbered through *The European Dream*, and was now ponderously changing direction between the castle and *The Mother Courage Kitchen*.

From his elevated throne Cocky Chicken spotted Daphne. Frank Babbitt the visionary supervisor had personally warned him. She was dressed all in blue, from her trainers to her skirt to her wide-necked T-shirt, her bare legs smooth and slender like drumsticks, separate from the crowd on the upslope of the moat-bridge at the entrance to the *Bavarian Schloss*.

She was ignoring him. She was turning her back and walking away from him.

With the unrivalled vigour of his greatest ironing-board era cartoons, Cocky Chicken clambered down from his throne. He steadied himself on the low fringe of the slow-moving float, then jumped, landing solidly on both foam-rubber feet. He flourished an elaborate farewell to Clucky, whose hands flew astonished to her fixed-grin beak. The audience gasped. Cocky turned side-on to the castle, drew

192

back his leading leg, and lowered his shoulder. He knew where he was going. He was the king, the come-back king of the action cartoon. Inanimate objects and all God's creatures would bend and sing to help him on his way.

The crowd moved apart like safety curtains in a single-screen cinema, and off Cocky went, urgently bouncily jogging towards the moat-bridge where he'd seen Frank's girl, evil to the core. She must be hiding inside the castle. He bounced up and over the hump-back of the bridge, under the stone-arched gateway, and there she was by the dark descending stair to the dank and dreary dungeons.

Cocky Chicken was going to catch hold of that wicked witch and roundly soundly box her ears, only just then he was grabbed by the elbow, spun around (*me! Cocky Chicken!*), and slammed against a pillar. The girl was running! She was leaving the castle, she was escaping!

Frank pinned Cocky where he was, then put into practice an important lesson learnt from the last time. He had to get Cocky away from the customers. He therefore bundled him upstairs to the *Ferdinand and Isabella Gallery* of significant European marriages. Then he leapt back down the stone staircase, at least two steps at a time, and put out the sign for *Seasonally Closed*.

He then had to bound back up, and chase Cocky twice round the gallery before catching him. He grabbed the chicken's red waistcoat and pulled him to a standstill. Then, with his bare hands, he ripped off Cocky's head. Above the collar of feathers those familiar independent eyes jittered after evidence of Daphne, bouncing off Frank as they went. 'You!'

'I saw her, Frankie, did you see her?'

'I should have guessed! How did Cocky get to be you?'

'Frank, you don't know the half of it.'

193

'Try me.'

'It was the way he walked. There was always something funny about the way he did the walk.'

Earlier in the day, making no allowances for the heat, Michael Miller had watched in tight-lipped fury as for the second morning in a row Cocky Chicken lost all flair for the silent chortle. It was a disgrace, and as supervising farmer he'd felt compelled to cut the performance short, ushering both chickens back towards the summer-house. He allowed them one last wave high and goodbye, then shut the two of them inside. After calming the disappointed audience, he opened the door again and closed himself in with the chickens. It was baking in there, and Cocky was already turning and pulling off his head.

'Fuck off,' she said. It was a girl, handsome and dark-haired. Just as Michael had always suspected, another impostor.

'Of course it was a girl,' Frank said, back up in the marriage gallery. 'We often have girls, you idiot. They're smaller and they move better.'

'She couldn't do the bounce.'

'You still didn't have to jump off the float, did you?'

'I saw the girl in blue, with the doll. It was Cocky to the rescue.'

Frank raised his fist, and scowled, but remembering the power in Michael's man-made hand he didn't actually hit him. From the animated classics Michael must have learnt that some people rose up and were heroes, and others didn't and were villains. Michael our saviour, as if everyone could be protected, even from mocked-up bombs. And it was then, in an unexpected moment of revelation, that Frank suddenly realised: if he saved absolutely everyone then they'd simply have to promote him. As for Daphne, she was nothing but a

194

troublemaker, just like the duck. Michael said: 'We're wasting time, Frank. We have to catch her.'

'*I* was going to say that!'

Frank would be the hero, saving every one of us. He puffed out his chest, and unclipped the radio from the lapel of his dogtooth jacket. Unnoticed, Michael replaced his Cocky head. Frank put in a call to the *Rathaus*. Not spitting, reassured that this was no plan of the duck's, he asked for a general alert instructing all *Yurayama* personnel to apprehend young women wearing blue, and also anyone carrying a Mickey Mouse doll.

'Are you sure?'

'These are the people who hate us, beyond all reason.'

'What about people wearing white?'

'It's not as widespread as that.'

'Are you feeling alright, Frank?'

'Never better. This is important.'

'We're actually quite busy with something else. Maybe you're still sick from the other day?'

They weren't going to do it. Frank fixed his jaw, and tossed his radio over the stone banisters. He undid his top button, and loosened his tie. He put his best foot forward, and balled his fists for the audition as solitary hero.

Poor old Daphne. I'd have liked to give her fair warning, but she was in *Yurayama*, and I was in *Disneyland Paris*. There was therefore nothing I could do for her. She wasn't allowed to be where I was, or the other way round. That was the law. I couldn't be with her, to help her, hold her, stop her from falling.

It wasn't just the law. She hadn't wanted us to be together, not after last night, but I was feeling our separation more tragically than that.

Relax. It's not the Sistine Chapel, it's *Disneyland Paris*.

Wandering into *Adventureland*, I saw a Frank Babbitt, frazzled and unsure as a park guest grilled him on what was real. He passed the guest over to a Michael Miller, quite certain, happily complacent. Once or twice I thought I saw Daphne, but that was impossible.

For a lunch of fun carbohydrates, and a plug for the hole in my tooth, I queued for a table at *Colonel Hathi's Pizza Outpost*. I ended up sharing with a divorcing couple from the Luxembourg fatlands, taking photographs of the last days of their marriage. Back home they felt something had gone missing, in their lives just generally, but during this farewell week of pilgrimage they'd made nearly enough purchases to chase that feeling away. They were considering giving it another go. Then they handed me their disposable camera, and I took aim at them across the table, sincerely cheek to cheek.

I was tempted to run off with the camera, and blamed it on food-poisoning. For some time now, in Disneyland Paris, I hadn't felt quite right. Distinctly odd, as a matter of fact, indignation fizzing inside me like something gastric. It was the infection of Frank's modern and universal duck, swelling, taking shape, threatening to make a scene. I wanted it out. I found an empty bench over by *Autopia*, and breathing deeply, I laid my hands on my rumbling, squeaking, quacking stomach.

Back at *Yurayama*, Daphne's common sense had dismissed the paranoid impression that Cocky Chicken in person was already in hot pursuit. All the same, it seemed wise to distance herself from the castle. She pushed under the ropes laid out for the continuing parade, and crossed *Gran Via 2000*, dodging between costumed dancers and rolling floats. *European Space Mission* would make a decent location B for Chang's tiny but significant bomb. Still clutching

196

the doll, Daphne therefore stepped out with undimmed confidence from the back of the parade-watching crowd, just beside the *Vienna Bakery*. She froze. Five or six red anoraks were milling by *The Lisbon Landslide*.

This was Daphne's first big mistake, forgetting that *Yurayama's* design was modelled on animated cartoons. Nothing was ever completely still, except for Daphne outside the *Vienna Bakery*. She made it so easy for Frank, who just then arrived from the direction of the parade. He tapped her lightly on the shoulder. 'Howdy.'

Daphne straightened and turned. She blew out her cheeks in relief. 'God, Frank, you frightened me! What's up?'

'I've changed my mind.'

Frank had never been able to tell when the duck was the rabbit in disguise, or the other way round. He was always the straight guy, befuddled, bemused. At the turnstiles he'd let Daphne in as if breaking the rules was the only valid exercise for his soul. In fact, he'd let the duck overpower him, with another of those fabulous plans custom-made to go horribly wrong.

He'd since remembered the mathematics, like a universal law. *Yurayama* was pure, innocent, inoffensive and well intentioned, harmless good fun for the family and a haven of pan-European optimism. He was therefore crazy to think of risking his career for a mean, corrupt, embittered, over-sophisticated, jealous, cynical, anti-European and elitist public nuisance. And an enemy of all children and all families, everywhere and all of the time. Long live the mouse.

Daphne was backing away. 'Us against them,' she said, holding up her fist. 'You wouldn't help us but you wouldn't report us. We're on the same side, remember?'

Frank followed her, step by step. Daphne put her finger

197

through the plastic ring in the middle of Mickey's back, gripping the doll itself with a straight arm like an engine she meant to ripstart. Frank took another step and Daphne spread her feet wide, for the balance. 'Don't come any closer. Stay where you are.'

'What are you doing?'

'I'll pull it. The plastic ring hits Mickey's back. Kaboom.'

'Fake bombs don't kaboom.'

'Does it look like a fake?'

'I don't get it. It was supposed to be funny.'

'It's a bomb, a real one. The cord's the detonator.'

'I don't think so,' Frank said. He laughed. When Daphne didn't join in, he rocked back and laughed louder. 'That wouldn't be very amusing, would it?'

'Want to find out? Distract your colleagues in the red anoraks. Then leave me alone.'

'You promised me fake, that's what you said. Imitation dynamite and hollow black bombs was a very funny idea.'

'Funny doesn't change anything.'

Hurting strangers was still the best mad way to get attention, because it always worked. Dressing up in chicken-suits and a cartoon bombing were very start-of-the-century, but aggressive irony was unlikely ever to change anything. Frank should have seen from the start that worse was always coming, only he'd been far too busy spinning his fists and leaping up and down, and backwards. Now, watching Daphne walk away, he could taste his own heart. Yet again the duck had quacked it all up.

Meanwhile, exclusively live, up on the inside balcony of the first floor of the castle, here he was with his new-found voice, squeaky and clean, the one, the only Cocky Chicken. Like cartoon characters everywhere he was physically without limit. Strong-legged, straight-eyed, dextrous, he needed only our help to crush the villains flat.

Cocky climbed up onto the rail of the banisters, and balled his feathered fists. He punched fresh air and stamped up and down, dangerously over-animated. He was quacky and all out of character, and this wasn't the self-possession we'd been led to expect from the chicken. Confused guests drifted away singly, in pairs, until it happened more quickly than that, Cocky's recent crowd breaking up like ice.

Daphne latched on to the queue for *European Space Mission*, shortened by the temporary draw of the parade. Frank joined the line immediately behind her. Bugger. The man just didn't know when to stop. More people joined the queue directly behind Frank, and already it was easier to carry on than go back. It was designed that way, and neither Frank nor Daphne could afford a scene in the middle of all these people. They shuffled forwards, tight-lipped, at this parade-time of day waiting not too long for the space-port, the allocation of an empty spaceship, the preparation side by side for orbit.

Up crawled the spaceship, slowly does it.

Daphne glanced sideways, just once. Then, looking straight ahead, she changed her position against the padded safety-restraint, dislodging *Save the Tiger*, showing off her bra-strap. It was ivory, almost white, but despite her smooth and luminous skin Frank was acting older than that now, and wiser, with a belated understanding of what it meant to be adult. It involved feeling at ease with women, and deferring to evident facts, however uninspiring, like the earlier he went to bed the less tired he woke up in the morning. Like the less he drank the longer he'd stay sober. The emergency of Daphne and the real bomb (or so she said)

199

had found out the inner man, practical, a little weary, suddenly too old for disgruntled bluster.

The glittery spaceship twitched to a halt, creaking and snorting before lift-off. Smoke and steam and docking-release noises, and a tannoyed robotic countdown. 10, 9, 8,

'Come on, Frank.' Daphne shrugged herself back into the T-shirt. 'What's the problem?'

7, 6, 5,

'This is the end, Daphne. Let it go.'

'Nobody gets hurt.'

4, 3, 2,

'We have to be more serious than this.'

Boom! Lift-off. For three and a half minutes they sped through the dark, often upside-down, at sixty mph through a hail of disintegrating space-station.

At the limits of the known universe, the spaceship slowed and docked and stopped. The safety-restraints disengaged with a hiss like air-brakes, Frank and Daphne pushing them off and away, stumbling along the platform, blinking out into the blinding afternoon light. Before Daphne could dream up anything nasty, that sly inner child again, Frank lunged for the Mickey Mouse. He grabbed its leg. He pulled. As a precaution, Daphne still had her finger inside the plastic ring. The cord unreeled its full length, then jarred, until all that stood between them was a foot of stretched white nylon.

'Bloody hell, Frank. Now look what you've gone and done.'

'Let go.'

'No. You let go.'

Daphne pulled hard and the doll snapped out of Frank's hands, flying a wide arc above their heads. Time. In mid-air, at the apex of its flight, the doll had all the time in the world.

Mickey turned and spread himself into free fall, smiling left and right, until a human hand in slow motion reached up for the catch, a woman's hand, Daphne's free hand not gripping the ring.

She caught the doll by the body, and held it away from her to stop the cord from reeling in. It hadn't even reached the *P* of *Pow!*, but Daphne's arms were shaking from the nearness of the miss, hands about a foot apart, the ring and the doll, the tight cord in between like a magic invisible stick. She had nowhere to run. Behind her, like the boundary of an arena, there was the dead-end of a curving wall, and in front of her there was Frank.

Watchful, wary, very carefully, Frank Babbit took off his jacket. He was going to get serious, even if no one else was, even without the relevant experience. He'd grown up like everyone else, besieged by advertising, and its contraction of every big idea for the business of any trivial purchase. It was so much easier to laugh it off, or to play at anger and do nothing, as if nothing really mattered. In other words, it was easier being the duck.

He sighed, and gently laid down his jacket on the swept gravel beside this exit to *European Space Mission*. He rolled up his sleeves, calmly expecting some help, especially after banishing the duck and acting the hero. So where was the ledge with the big red rock on top, hanging in the balance for Daphne? Why weren't God's creatures answering the call to help him on his way? The jacket, then. Frank wasn't fussy. His dogtooth jacket surrendered on the ground should take on a life of its own, outer not inner, and sweep itself up to fight beside him. Ha-ha, Daphne, you evil little vixen, two against one.

Frank wiped both hands down the front of his white shirt, appraising the string tight in Daphne's outstretched hands, and also the doll's rigid, stitched smile, no help to anyone.

'It's failed actors in animal suits, and baby children,' he said, offering her one last chance. 'I don't believe you'd do it.'

'That doesn't make it not true,' Daphne said, 'just because you don't believe it.'

'It's stupid. Stupid and childish.'

He stepped forward, slapped the doll and Daphne's laughably frail arms aside, and then circled her neck with his broad, swelling hands. He lifted her clean off her feet. Her eyes goggled but she kept the string rigid at all times, her lowered outspread arms the width of an unhooked fish.

Louder than the distant parade-music, the rumble of an oncoming crowd flooded both sides of the *Breitling Orbital Balloon Challenge*. Frank was now holding Daphne off the ground by her ankles, shaking her up and down. Magic markers and unused condoms tumbled from her canvas bag, and her entrance ticket, and a photo of me as a boy with my mother. Then the whole bag, over her head and onto the ground. Her skirt flipped. You could see her glossy pants!

Frank stopped shaking, and very precisely he rested the top of Daphne's head against the gravel. He was going to spin her forcefully in a clockwise direction until she entered the earth like a drill.

That is, if only Cocky Chicken hadn't bounced up from his blindside at exactly the same moment, and whacked him in the ribs with a shovel.

'CLANG!'

Frank, still upright, though shuddering from his toes to the top of his head, let go of Daphne's ankles, and she collapsed on the ground in a heap. From his long working life, Cocky knew very well that one clang didn't make a cartoon. CLANG!

202

Now Frank staggered and now he clutched his ribs, and now he fell down. Oof. The side of his face pimpled with small stones from the sandy gravel.

'You idiot!' he croaked, raising his head and coughing away a *Lilla's Tortillas* wrapper inches from his nose. The litter taunted him, sticking out its tongue, retreating in flamenco with full castanets. 'You complete and total idiot! This is the same person who dressed up as Cocky!'

At this point I could have helped. I could have saved them all, including the future of the park itself, except I wasn't there. I was trying out the rollercoasters in *Disneyland Paris*, one after the other, hoping to be distracted by their maximum excitement for minimum effort, like drugs. I queued up for cars and was strapped into seats, each time anticipating the fantastic sensory attack I'd fallen for only yesterday. Here it comes: all thought lost in the white-knuckled and neckless up-and-down, the heavy run of steel wheels, and speed in my ears like the frothing outdoors.

With the exception of *Star Tours*, which gave me motion sickness despite being simulated, I was rarely distracted, partly because the end of each ride always led to a shop. There was no escaping the flat-earth Disneyworld in which all creation, concrete and abstract, could equally be recreated as commodity. This assumption was everywhere, permeating everything, and maddeningly, instinctively, I felt like I wanted to protest. I was inspired to do something stupid.

Though not yet, however shaken I was by these severe inside-out raids by the duck. I heard an explosion. But then later I heard it again. It was the regular explosive lift-off of *Space Mountain*, though at least once it almost seemed muffled, as if heard through a pile of soft toys.

Telling myself to keep calm (talking to myself!), I joined the back of the queue for *The Temple of Peril*. This was the only thrill-ride I still hadn't done, an outside rollercoaster themed round a plundered Aztec temple. I spent the next hour queuing, not calming down, reading and forgetting T-shirts, learning nothing from trademarks and slogans, my private fury mounting just generally at the modern world. Before I could squawk my protest, out loud there and then, I was strapped into a runaway mining car. It ran away with me. By the time I caught up again, breathless, the cars had dipped and slowed. Working towards the ride's climax, we set off on a long upward haul on ticking undertrack chains to the highest, most potentially energetic point on the gleaming iron rails.

It was there, right at the top, out in the high and open air, for a split second, half of it tilted up, half down, that at last I saw it. And then half a second later it was off and away again, round into the hole of my stomach and a sideways loop-the-loop.

But I'd definitely seen it, up at the top of *The Temple of Peril*. I went straight from the exit back to the entrance, and re-joined the hour-long line. I wanted to see it again.

At *Yurayama*, because it was Cocky Chicken, a crowd had gathered, expecting to be amused in the amusement-park. Cocky was making up his mind about Daphne, hands on hips, elbows forward, fingers back, the shovel propped upright against his convex waistcoat. He was tapping a foam-rubber foot. Clearly, for anyone to see, the dangerous girl in blue was holding a sacred doll without the required devotion. She was stretching the cord out tight from Mickey's back. She wasn't letting him speak! In *Yurayama*, everyone gets to speak.

'Stay back!' Daphne lifted the doll and the outstretched cord high above her head. 'I'll let it go!'

Cocky took a double-fisted grip on the handle of the

shovel, and lifted it like a bat. He swung it in a fast arc, missed, and was pulled sideways by the shovel's momentum. He swung it back again, missed again, now toppling that way, dragged off-balance by the blade.

Frank tackled him head-first from behind, and Cocky fell with a soft thump, like a soft toy, though dropping his shovel, which slid and clattered away. The encircling audience moved in closer. Cocky was still down, and he'd lost some feathers, and usually he recovered more quickly than this.

Fearing another riot, Frank made a big show of helping him up, dusting him off, making an exhibition of his supervisor's matchless Lunch-and-Learn smile. Cocky shook his over-sized feathered head as if dazed. He was permanently looking to the right, because the fall had knocked him out of alignment, and all Michael could now see was the black insides of the head.

'My head's funny,' he said, forgetting in the dark to do the voice. 'I can't see where I am.' He went to adjust it.

'Stop!' Daphne said. 'Cocky, I have something to give you, a present.'

'*Will I like it?*'

'I think so.'

She placed the doll in one of his hands, and the ring attached to the outstretched cord in the other. 'Don't let go,' she said, pushing his hands apart. 'Keep it tight.' The small ring was slippery in Cocky's three-fingered feathered hand, but he did as he was told and managed to keep it tight.

Daphne should already have been running. Frank grabbed her by the wrist.

'Ow!' She turned and twisted, but he gritted his teeth and didn't let go. 'Violence! Rape! Murder!', but this time she wasn't disguised as a chicken. #*!@#! She tried again, in French. '*Sacré maroon! Gendarme! Air France! Avec!*', but a young girl in unstaged trouble was another of those outside realities no one wanted to believe, and today's visitors had spent good money on expensive tickets to believe in something else. They hurried onwards through *Tomorrow is Today!*, or back to the castle, averting their eyes from this unlicensed spectacle in between.

'It's all gone dark,' Michael complained. 'I need to adjust my head. I'm going to put this thing down.'

'Don't move!' It was Frank, loud and urgent, and still grappling with Daphne. 'Michael, stay exactly where you are! There's a huge red rock right above your head, trembling on a ledge. Move an inch and it falls!'

Cocky Chicken stood quite still, frozen, looking alertly to the right. In one feathered hand he held the doll. In the other, threatening to slide between his three clumsy fingers, he had the ring attached to the end of the unreeled cord.

Frank pulled Daphne into him by the wrist, pushing his face in close to hers. She stopped struggling. 'Tell me it's not a bomb.' It was a fake bomb and this was another funny sabotage, except this time the joke was on him.

'*A bomb?*' It was Cocky again.

'The rock, Michael. It's quivering. Don't even speak!'

Frank stared hard at Daphne, and she stared straight back, blocking him at the defiant limit of her eyes. It was a bomb, it wasn't. She believed it was. She was daring him to believe the same.

'It would have to be very small,' Frank said, 'if it was real.'

'Big enough.' Daphne felt superior, righteous, high-chinned. 'I arranged it with a veteran of the Vietnam war, in the city of Paris. It's definitely the real thing.'

'*How's the rock?*' Cocky Chicken still hadn't moved.

'For God's sake, Michael,' Frank said. 'There is no rock. I made it up.'

206

'*You expect me to believe that?*'

From between his slippery, clumsy, feathery fingers, out slid the plastic ring.

Pow!

'Grab it!' Daphne moved first, her wrist still trapped, dragging Frank towards Cocky, and the Mickey Mouse doll, which he'd now dropped, upending it in the dust. Unsighted in the heavy costume, Cocky fell over, trapping the doll beneath him.

Right Between

Frank made a lunge for it, not daring to let go of Daphne. All he had to do was grab the cord before the ring hit Mickey Mouse in the back. There, he could see it, moving in the gravel beneath Cocky and all his costume. He went down on his knees, but close to the ground Daphne bit into his thumb, her teeth mashing through to the bone.

'Aaaaagh!'

The Whiskers!

I hadn't invented or imagined it. Up at the highest, most pronounced curve of the gleaming steel track of *The Temple of Peril*, the Walt Disney Company had made a mistake. If you don't believe me you can go seven days a week all year round to *Disneyland Paris*, and see for yourself. Keep your eyes open in the split second between up and down, high above the plundered Aztec temple: there's a view up there of an unthemed France beyond the park. There are farms to be seen, and flat gridlocked fields, a straight grey road, and a tractor and trailer chugging slowly along. They haven't closed off their world.

As the car swooped down into the double belly of the corkscrew loop I scrunched up my eyes and beamed my teeth. I whooped. Here was the evidence, easy to miss, which disproved the idea that Disney didn't make mistakes, that a corporation could uniquely gauge the moods and desires of the people. As if no manipulation was ever involved, and only the grace of infallible judgement. Keep your eyes open. At the top of *The Temple of Peril* in *Disneyland Paris* there's a Disney-defeating oversight. Unfortunately, as a direct consequence of the designs of the experience, most people don't keep open their eyes.

I rode *The Temple* again and again, until the ten o'clock closing-time was nearer than the estimated length of the day's last queue. That left me almost an hour, which I kept for a final tour of the park, stopping here and there to watch the sun go down on another day in small-town America at the turn of the century, and in Africa, Arabia, the Caribbean, the jungle, in the land of the future, and of fairy-tales and make-believe, for children big and small. I was several times overtaken by the same ragged families stumbling on towards *Honey I Shrunk the Audience* or *Peter Pan's Flight*, the children too tired to cry, Mickey ears askew and light-sabres trailing gullies in the dust.

Another day had seen enough, and as the light faded I sat down exhausted on the slatted wooden porch of *The Silver Spur Steakhouse*, with a view of *Big Thunder Mountain* and the *Thunder Mesa Mercantile Building*. Behind me, the restaurant was slowly extinguishing the wildness of the West, ending the evening's service with a sigh of waitresses laced into southern-comfort ballgowns. From *The Lucky Nugget Saloon* came drifting the wavering farewell of a harmonica lament.

I took off my running-shoes. Then my damp black socks, placing my pale feet either side of my *Disneyland Paris* plastic carrier-bag. I pushed back against the outside wall of the restaurant, and stretched the elasticated neck of the orange *Bug's Life* T-shirt that at some stage during the day I'd bought to freshen myself up. As I rested my head against the stone wall, it was cushioned by the plastic adjuster at the back of my red *Disneyland Paris* baseball cap. One size fits all.

I'd located their basic mistake, but I'd also made my purchases.

Disneyland Paris was welcoming and safe and clean. Small girls in beribboned Minnie ears could often be seen skipping. Parents in many languages laughed at their own laughter, and since 1992 more than sixty million Europeans had come here wanting whatever there was to be had. This is what they wanted, and they didn't want discarded condoms or mutinous characters or a trail of possible bombs, though no comparable statistics were available.

I pushed up the peak of the baseball cap, and rubbed my eyes. I felt like a coward, a secret convert to the lie that *Disneyland Paris* was nothing but harmless fun. If you think otherwise, like Daphne, then someone somewhere will laugh at you. *Lighten Up!* No one wants that.

As for what I did want, in a perfect world I'd somehow be able to stop, and live permanently at the top of *The Temple of Peril*, at the highest possible point, always about to dip. Up there, in that gap in the split between the split second, I could see my way out to an ending immune from all this, me and Daphne happily ever after in an unthemed bed. We'd laugh a lot, or not. We'd provide our own entertainment. But then half a second later I'm off and accelerating, round into the hole of my stomach and looping the loop to this other ending, alone at twilight, cap, *Bug's Life*, bag, feet, abject on the porch of *The Silver Spur Steakhouse*, no Daphne anywhere, to the tune of the lamentable West.

I tugged at the peak of the cap, pulling it low. It was all

over, like in the fourth panel of four, and I'd missed the happy ending I'd dreamt for Daphne. I'd go back to Paris. I'd take the train to *Yurayama*. I'd find her and follow her, because any other ending had to be better than this, even a theme-park ending with a shop at the exit, and Daniel and Daphne tableware.

Daphne and Frank both liked to say we only live once. Both of them were wrong. For cartoon characters, there's always a second chance.

I lifted my hand from Daphne's breast. In the rebounded light from the hospital carpark, I climbed off the bed and padded back shoeless from my side to hers. She was awake, but couldn't move from whatever position I chose to place her in.

I took away all her pillows except one. Her head and gauze-covered neck-brace and all the rest of her were now in a single straight line along the bed. By taking a firm grip on the cotton of the hospital smock, at the shoulder and hip furthest away, I pulled her over until she was balanced on her side, meaning her nearer hip and shoulder. Both her arms were bent at the elbow, offering out the bandaged hands to the side of the bed at right angles. I knelt down, and looked into her open eyes. They were wide and bright and brown, and this time the brightness was fear, perhaps, or confusion.

But more likely it was a dare.

The drip, slowly slowly dripping dry, the transparent bag sucking itself in like cheeks, was hanging from a hook on a metal pole slotted into a circular base, on wheels. I rolled it to a safer distance, the plastic tubing stretching tight to the map of veins on the inside of Daphne's arm. I padded back to my side of the bed, climbed up, lay down behind her, breathed in the smell of her hair.

The tips of my undamaged fingers, with a memory of their own, paddled over to Daphne's unbandaged breast. Inevitably, the palm and the heel of the hand followed along. In this new sideways position there was a definite weight there, which I could lift, and lower. I closed my eyes, reassured she wasn't a boy, envisioning her weighted breast. Lifting, lowering, in black, in white, from every conceivable angle.

Family had more meaning because the panels were harder to close. Family had memory, and didn't just stop. It had less white space, always coming back. Her neck had a mentholated smell. I wiped my palm dry on the sheet, because Daphne wasn't the only one with a scheme to save our souls.

Between my thumb and forefinger I lifted up the single sheet, and beneath it her pale-green patient's gown was fixed at the back with bows, one at the neck, one at the waist. Below that, the material had twisted to the front. She was. On her naked and rounded and left and upper buttock, and more towards the centre than not, Daphne had a big red boil. If Sleeping Beauty. In modern times, we have to push further for the same ending, to arrive in the beatified place.

I unfastened the lower of the two bows, needing both hands because it had tightened when I pulled her over into position. It loosened, unravelled, and I cleared the gown away with the flat of my hands. I pressed myself against her, lightly at first, because in many ways I was sorry, wishing it wasn't for the best, and that no special virtue attached to reality. When these days amid so much pretending, pain seems the only. And the easiest.

From close to her stitches, between the iodine and the bruising, Daphne produced a continuous high-pitched whine, like something electrical overlooked in the dark.

This wasn't a cartoon experience.

But still, if I hadn't already wasted my wishes, I'd have

wished with my final wish, no, not that quite yet, but first of all that pain wasn't the most common ground for meeting with the realness of the world.

She had that angry boil on the downsweep of her tensed and trembling buttock.

What would it matter. No one was looking.

It was a test, like always. The door opened and on came the light, and curious in the doorway a puzzled nurse. Then Aunt Lillian in a motherly flurry to the head of the bed, where, without thinking, I'd already feigned sleep, not moving, not weeping, like an idiot.

A NOTE ON THE AUTHOR

Richard Beard is the author of two previous novels, *X20* and *Damascus*. Until recently he lived at Brookleaze, not far from Midsomer Norton rugby club.